BOOK 3

GHOST HUNTRESS
the reason

MARLEY GIBSON

*To Nicole —
Happy hunting!
Marley Gibson :)*

GRAPHIA

Houghton Mifflin Harcourt
Boston   New York   2010

www.hmhbooks.com

Text set in Bembo

Library of Congress Cataloging-in-Publication Data
is on file.

ISBN 978-0-547-15095-6

Manufactured in the United States of America

DOM 10 9 8 7 6 5 4 3 2 1
4500220226

ACKNOWLEDGMENTS

To my publishing team: Deidre Knight, best agent on the planet, and her fabulous assistant, Elaine Spencer; Julia Richardson, best editor on the planet, and her awesome assistant, Julie Bartynski; Karen Walsh, Stephanie McLaughlin, Barbara Fisch, and Sarah Shealy, the best publicists on the planet; and Carol Chu, the best graphic designer on the planet. And huge thanks to Betsy Groban, the most supportive publisher on the planet.

To my family for their love and unquestioning support, especially when I've needed it the most: Joe and Lizanne Harbuck; Jennifer, Dave, Sarah, Josh, and Stephanie Keller; and Jeff Harbuck. And just because you're listed last, Jeff, doesn't mean I appreciate you any less . . . just going chronologically. LOL!

To my paranormal family for their support and encouragement: Maureen Wood, Patrick Burns, Dave Schrader, Chris Fleming, Donn Shy (the real one), Kathryn Wilson, Fran Spencer, Delia Summerfield, Michael and Marti Parry, Bill Murphy, Andi LaFreniere, Bill Chappell, Mark and Debby Constantino, Stacey Jones, John Zaffis, Shannon and Jeff Sylvia, Marlo Scott, and Dawn Epright, who does an awesome Kendall Moorehead impression.

To my legal team: Anna Osterberg and Kelly Reed. Thanks

for helping me get through a very trying and challenging time in my life.

To my critique partners: Wendy Toliver and Jenn Echols. Can't believe I didn't use your talents on this one, but thanks for having my back, *chicas!*

To my Bunnies: Melly-Mel, Kristen, Louisa, Maria, Rocki, Kresley, Gena, Jill, and Pamela. Love you, ladies . . . wish we all lived in the same area. And to the WACs, Jess and Char: can't say enough about what the two of you mean to me.

Thanks to everyone who's reading the series—please keep it up and let me know what you think!

*To William and Alec Burns, my summer travel buddies, and
to their dad, Patrick, for his amazing love and support*

All that we see or seem
Is but a dream within a dream.

—*Edgar Allan Poe*

CHAPTER ONE

It's NOT EVERY DAY YOU HAVE A PREMONITION of your own freakin' demise. But that's just what happened to me, Kendall Moorehead. It's been almost three months since my dream— or vision, or whatever you want to call it—of me, well, like, dying. I know. Skeeved me out too.

I mean, since my whole psychic awakening thing after moving from Chicago to Radisson, Georgia, back in August, I've had a lot of strange dreams and seen a lot of apparitions and stuff. I even dreamed about my boyfriend before I met him in person. But to have this precognition thing where I saw myself bruised, unconscious, and bleeding to death . . . not exactly your typical day in the life of a seventeen-year-old.

Still, I can't shake the image. And I can't deny that it's rattled me more than a little bit.

Other than the whole wacked dream thing, everything else is going pretty sweet in my life. I had my birthday back on December 22 (solstice baby, as my friend Loreen Woods likes to remind me), and my parents got me a combined birthday/

Christmas present (like so many other Capricorns are cursed with) of a brand-new Honda Fit. It looks like a fat blue bullet. Well, the marketing materials from the dealership paint it as Blue Sensation Pearl, but I digress.

My awesome boyfriend, Jason Tillson, bought me this really cool hematite bracelet for my birthday to match the one I had given him for Christmas—we sort of coordinated the whole thing and special-ordered it since my b-day is the twenty-second. Now we're bracelet buddies (LOL!) and have a forever symbol of our connection, love, and dedication to each other. See, hematite absorbs any negativity and bad energy that's out to get you. Not that Jason totally believes in all of this, but he knows how important it is to me to be protected at all times from the spirits who knock on my door on a daily basis. I haven't exactly told him about this visionary dream thing of my death. He'd totally lose his shit if I did. He's protective enough about his twin sister, Taylor; Lord knows how he'd be if he thought I was in some sort of imminent danger. Still, if something in the universe is gunning for my life, I need all the protection I can get from hematite, the holy water Father Massimo blessed for me, and Jason as my bodyguard. I suppose I'll have to tell him about the dream . . . eventually.

I'd rather not think about it, though.

Breathe in. Breathe out. There. That helps.

So, between hanging with Jason, doing the whole ghost-hunting thing with Celia, Taylor, and Becca, and keeping up with all of my classes—don't even get me going on how stupid calculus is—not to mention the Radisson High School spring formal, I'm one busy chick.

I don't have time to dwell on, dissect, or otherwise occupy my time with a fleeting night vision of something that may or may not happen to me.

I have to focus on the present. After all, it's the only thing I can control. Besides, it's a nice Saturday and I've got a lot going on today.

I'm walking through Radisson—which is starting to grow on me, although I still miss my Chicagoland—on my way to Divining Woman. That's Loreen's store, where she sells all sorts of metaphysical stuff and where she's let me hang out a shingle, so to speak, to do psychic readings and such. I look around me at the bare-limbed trees just starting to show tiny green buds as we come out of winter this February. I've got two people coming in for tarot readings at the store and I'm also going to finish up this online training for energy healing and attunement studies. No, I'm not turning into some kind of freak of nature. It really works.

A cool breeze rustles around me, causing me to pull the zipper of my black hoodie up under my chin. Most of my fellow townspeople are still wearing fleece, wool, or down coats, like they're at some ski resort in Jackson Hole, Wyoming. Not me, the hardy Midwesterner and survivor of many lake-effect storms. It takes a lot more than a stiff breeze to make me dive for the gloves and scarves. A mere chilly day like this is nothing. I suppose at some point I'll grow accustomed to the warmer southern climate. At least I'm starting to be accepted here for the most part, making a lot of friends at school and throughout the town.

Like the person waving at me now.

"Hi there, Kendall," a tiny woman calls out from the garden area in front of the antebellum mansion to my left.

"Hi, Mayor Shy," I say with a wave. "Are you coming into the store for another treatment?"

Donn Shy, a petite woman with long, straight golden blond hair, stands and brushes her hands off on the thighs of her designer jeans. She's one of my newest clients at Divining Woman; she started with a psychic reading, then worked up to tarot, and now, finally, she's taking a whack at my attunement healing.

I learned with my psychic intuition that her name was once Donna Cheyenne, but she changed it to Donn Shy in the early seventies when she was the lead singer of a go-go type band in California. How she ended up in Radisson is still beyond my abilities to understand, as there's sort of a curtain surrounding most info on her. Still, she's standing there with a pair of hedge clippers in her fist and a bag of potting soil next to her. Imagine that, the mayor of the town is outside doing her own yard work and not paying a bunch of minions to do it. Right, like the mayor of Chicago would do that! Not! What a difference between large and small towns.

She adjusts her stylish wire-rimmed glasses on the bridge of her nose. "I'd like to come in and see you if you have the time, Kendall. I'm still having those back pains, so I'll definitely need more energy healing. It seemed to work the last time you did it."

With a nod, I say, "Just lemme know and we'll get it taken care of." It's not every day that the mayor of your town comes to *you* for help. But then again, Radisson's not your normal city. It's relatively small, an hour east of Atlanta, and it's rich with Civil War history, full of gorgeous old houses from a time long past and a plethora of ghosts and spirits to keep me and my fellow ghost huntresses busy every weekend. Mayor Shy's house is the second-largest and second-oldest house in Radisson, with long, tall columns in the front of the mansion and a wraparound porch complete with white rockers. Of course, my best friend and neighbor, Celia Nichols, has the biggest house in town, since her dad is rolling in dough from owning the Mega-Mart conglomerate.

With a hand on the small of her back, the mayor winces. "I'd best come round tomorrow, if that's okay."

I nod. "Sure thing. We'll work on the specific areas you're having trouble with."

"It's so odd," she says. "I have no idea what I did to cause this."

"Maybe the yard work?" I suggest.

She waves me off with her hand. "I do this all the time. This is more of a pressure, like someone's pressing on my nerves."

I'm certainly no medical doctor and won't pretend to give a diagnosis. I do know that Mayor Shy went to see Dr. Murphy, who my mom works for as a staff nurse, and he couldn't find anything wrong with the mayor. Nothing on the X-rays to show a strain or tear. A follow-up visit to a chiropractor in Atlanta turned up nothing more. That's why Donn Shy called Loreen, who referred her to me. It would be wicked cool if I solved something with attunement activation that the medical community couldn't.

As Mayor Shy continues to tell me about her excruciating back pain, my eye is drawn away from her and up to the top of the mansion. I swear I think I see a woman standing at the small attic window, gazing down at me. I blink hard into the morning sun and lift my hand over my eyes to get a better look. There's no woman there now. However, the curtain moves back into place as if someone had been there. Must be one of the mayor's maids or something. Although I don't think it was. In my world and considering what I see with my gift, when I spot someone I don't always know if I'm dealing with the living or the dead.

"You all right, Kendall?" the mayor asks.

"Yes, ma'am. I just thought I saw someone in your attic."

Mayor Shy harrumphs. "There's no telling what it is. Everyone says this place is haunted. Just like every other building in Radisson. You should know that."

It's no secret that my friends and I have gotten phenomenal evidence of the paranormal in this town as well as helped several lost spirits on to their final resting place in the light. It amazes me how pretty much everyone just accepts that there are ghosts and spirits here. Like the trees are around us. Like the pavement that cuts through town.

"Maybe my team and I should come investigate the property?"

Mayor Shy flips her long hair behind her ears and then places her hands on her hips. "Anytime you can work me into your schedule, I'd appreciate it. Maybe you can contact Mayer and find out where the hell he left the key to the safety-deposit box before he cashed out on me." Her soft laugh makes me smile.

Her husband, Mayer Holt, was the mayor of the town before my family and I moved here. Yeah, Mayor Mayer. How funny is that? Not very, 'cause he, like, keeled over from a heart attack last summer. The deputy mayor moved his family to Ocala, Florida, so the city council asked the widow to step in. That's how Donn became mayor of Radisson. Not exactly a position she'd sought, but she seems to be handling it quite well.

The hairs on the back of my neck are raised and prickly—which is hard for them to do, since my hair is so long. Nonetheless, something's giving me the willies. I don't know if it's the woman I saw in the window or the general sense of unease on this property. It's like there's something . . . *off* . . . inside the mansion. Restless souls displeased with the current occupancy. Or perhaps still troubled with their own problems that they haven't given up to the light. I'm definitely getting a sense of a stirring within and anxiety for those that live here. Maybe that explains the mayor's current physical ailment. Although I can't be sure until I get my group here to investigate.

I swallow hard at the uneasiness clogging my throat. "I'll talk to the team and see when we can set up something." Celia is so good at fielding requests from people, answering our website e-mails, and booking our investigations. Plus, she's been salivating to get into the mayor's mansion ever since we were walking back from Stephanie Crawford's New Year's Eve party last month and Celia's EMF detector started going off like mad. Yeah, I love Celia, but she is a geek to the core. I mean, taking ghost-hunting equipment to social events? Seriously?

I had mild curiosity at the time when Celia noted the readings, but I've got much more now. With one more sideways glance at the top of the mansion, I see the flimsy white curtain move again. Someone is most certainly up there watching me converse with the mayor.

I say goodbye to Mayor Shy and turn in the direction of Divining Woman, but I lift my eyes to the window a final time. Clearly, I see the face of a woman looking down with a steely glare.

Her emotions rush at me, knocking me a little with the extent of her displeasure.

Just then, my spirit guide, Emily, appears before me, translucent and frowning terribly. Her lips are parted and her brow is furrowed.

Stay away from her, Emily says inside my head.

"Why?" I ask out loud.

Stay away.

Emily's another one who's overprotective of me. Between my mom and dad, Loreen, Father Mass, Jason, of course, and Emily, I have all protection bases covered. Still . . . Emily's never seemed so distraught or insistent.

Don't ignore me, Kendall.

The woman in the window drops the curtain one more time and disappears. As does Emily. God, isn't anything easy for me? Nope. Not when you're psychic. Just part of the circus that is my life.

Emily's warning. The spirit's stare. I know she and I are destined to come head to head.

With a long sigh, I mutter, "Here we go again."

Chapter Two

"Sarah, you've outdone yourself," my dad exclaims after dinner that night.

"Yeah, Mom," my little sister, Kaitlin, echoes, waving her napkin in the air. "That fried chicken was better than KFC."

Mom laughs, but I roll my eyes.

"Gack, Kaitlin. How can you compare Mom's afternoon of slaving over the stove to make us good old homemade fried chicken with pulling up to a window and paying four ninety-nine for processed potatoes and various parts?"

Dad snickers. "Tell us what you really think, sweetie."

I laugh too, trying so hard to grow out of my slightly spoiled Chicago snobbery I've had most of my life. I'm sorry, but nothing compares to a home-cooked meal like this. This really has nothing to do with manufactured chicken products at all, though. My energy has been completely out of whack today, and I know it. Loreen commented on my auras shifting like a rainbow of color. The psychic reading I did for Fran Spencer from the drugstore went completely haywire because I kept being interrupted by my own personal premonitions instead of staying focused on helping Ms. Spencer locate her lost cockatoo. My total unease continues to revolve around this impending sense of doom I feel. I keep trying to ask Emily about it—about the dream and how she says it's my future—but she's being so ambiguous that it's sincerely pissing me off. Of course, Celia would tell me that the mere existence of and connection with ghosts and spirits is vague, so I shouldn't be surprised when Emily is so standoffish. Still . . . I just don't feel like myself. And a little niggle inside tells me it also has something to do with the lingering presence I sensed at Mayor Shy's house this morning.

I sigh deeply and long. The chicken battle is ovah!

Mom picks up on my unease and reaches over to take my hand. "Is everything okay at school, Kendall?"

I wipe my mouth with my napkin and try not to fiddle with the edges of it. "Everything's cool. I've just . . . um, got a lot of assignments d0, especially in calculus, and Celia and I are working on some extra credit for computer class. Things are cruising along just fine."

Furrowing her brow, Mom isn't having any of it. "Look, sweetie, you've been quieter than usual these last few weeks. And especially since you got home today. You walk around the house like you're tiptoeing on eggshells, and you seem skittish whenever Kaitlin's playing her video games or I make loud sounds in the kitchen. Is something going on with your . . . you know . . . your abilities?"

I glance over at Dad and see him raise an eyebrow in my

mother's direction. He's as shocked as I am that she's actually accepted my psychicness finally. (Only took a few months; several visits to the Episcopal priest; and a battery of blood, physical, and psych tests in Atlanta.)

I look into her soft eyes, warm with concern for her older child. Should I tell her about the vision? Should I warn her about what possibly looms in my future? If I do, I'll surely be locked inside my room until I'm thirty-five—rightly so! I want to be honest, though. Hiding secrets from the ones you love isn't the way to go in life. I've certainly learned that through my awakening and all the probs Mom and I have worked through together.

Before I can force the words out, my sister jumps in.

"She's been sleepwalking," Kaitlin pipes up through a mouthful of lime Jell-O.

"What?"

"Seriously," Kaitlin repeats. "I hear it all the time."

"That's not me, dork. That's Emily."

My sister screws up her nose. "Your imaginary friend?"

"She's not imaginary. She's real. She talks to me all the time." At thirteen, Kaitlin doesn't buy into much that I've got going as her big sister. All she cares about is the latest show on Cartoon Network, making sure her Wii games are up to date, and hanging with her friends playing soccer. Just wait until *she* experiences *her* awakening. I mean, it's sure to happen, right? Look at me. This stuff runs in families . . . or so Loreen tells me.

Mom steps in. "Now, now, girls. Not at the dinner table."

Kaitlin's typical brattiness aside, I need to assure my parents that I'm all right. At least until I can figure out exactly what's going on. "I'm totally not sleepwalking. I'm fine. I've just got a lot on my plate, you know? I promise, if there's anything going on that you need to know about, I'll tell you."

Does it count as a lie if I have my fingers crossed under the table?

Dad stands and gathers our plates to carry them to the sink. "You have a good head on your shoulders, Kendall. We trust you. And you know you can tell us anything."

"Yes, Dad." I hang my head for a moment and stare at my crossed fingers. Maybe I should let my 'rents in on my vision.

Emily materializes in front of me with sad eyes. I'll overlook the fact that she's chosen to appear to me in the middle of the kitchen table, since she's a ghost. Things like tables, chairs, and walls have no effect on her.

What is it? I ask her in my head.

"It's best to keep your visions to yourself at this point."

Why?

"The future is often clouded."

But you told me the dream was real.

"I'm doing what I can to prevent it . . ."

With that, Emily reaches a translucent hand out to me. I can almost feel her fingers on my face, but I know it's not real. Then she fades away as quickly as she appeared.

"Wait!" I shout out.

Kaitlin jumps in her chair. "There she goes again. Talking to the air."

"Now, Kaitlin," my dad fusses. "Kendall?"

I swallow hard. "No prob, Dad. Emily was just, er, messing with me." When I hear our front doorbell, I push out of my chair and stand up. "That's Jason. He's coming over to study."

"Okay, dear," Mom says and then turns to attack the stack of dishes in the sink.

I've literally been saved by the bell. This time.

"I was born to kiss you."

When Jason says this I can't help pushing him away and laughing totally hard at him. "Have you been reading romance novels?" I ask cheekily.

He rolls aside and shoves our abandoned calculus books toward the foot of my bed. We've been making out like crazy for the past ten minutes, not even thinking about vectors, antiderivatives, or quadratic approximation.

Jason twists one of my long, loose curls around his index finger. "Don't laugh at me, Kendall. I love kissing you. You have great lips."

I feel the blush from the roots of my hair to the tips of my socked feet. This has become our study ritual. He comes over, we pore over the textbook for about an hour, and then all thoughts of facts and figures are out the window when he starts making out with me.

"You have awesome lips too," I say, wanting to giggle behind the words. Thing is, Jason and I are nuts, beans, and crackers about each other and I don't care how goofy anything I say sounds when we're together like this. I never thought I'd ever have a boyfriend who totally accepted me for all I am. Jason truly is too good to be true.

"Ouch!" he squeaks out. "Why'd you pinch me?"

I shine him a toothy grin. "To make sure you're real."

He smiles too. "As real as you are."

His blue eyes are dark with his desire for me. I don't need to be psychic to know that he'd like to take this relationship further. However, he's a gentleman—a Southern one, at that—and he isn't pushing me or making me feel like *that* is a step we *have* to take. For the time being, macking on each other as much as we can is pretty damn close to paradise.

Jason pulls me to him again, bringing our chests together as our lips meet. Yeah, maybe we were born to kiss each other. The energy between us is like electricity, and I feel like Swoony McSwoonerton every time I'm in his presence.

At least Emily's got the decency to give us space tonight. She's usually going all parental on my ass, telling me that Jason and I kiss way too much. Can one ever really kiss her boyfriend too much?

So we roll around for the next few minutes kissing all over each other, holding hands, and embracing. I'm so into him, loving the—well, the loving. This is what being a teenager is all about, isn't it? Not thoughts of death and dying. I relax more into Jason's arms, letting my worries cascade off my shoulders like water over Niagara Falls. Deep, soft kisses soothe and heal, erasing all doubt and worry of things that *might* be in the future.

I gasp into Jason's kiss when my mind's eye begins to home in on a misty vision before me. It's a guy whose face isn't quite clear. He's leaning toward me like *he's* going to kiss me. I can't make out the details of him, but his brown eyes shine at me. Who is this? Where did this come from? Is this some sort of premonition, like when I saw Jason before I met him?

I jerk away and stare straight into Jason's eyes.

"What's wrong?" he asks with concern written all over his face.

What does this mean? Are Jason and I going to break up? Are we not going to be together forever? I mean, I know we're young and stuff, but I don't see me with anyone other than him.

Hot tears begin to sting my eyes as I dwell on the possibility of losing Jason. Who was the guy with the brown eyes? Does he have something to do with this future where I die?

My hands cover my mouth to contain the choked sob.

Quickly, Jason sits up and puts his hands on my shoulders. "Kendall! Don't do this to me. What's going on? Are you okay?"

I lean my head onto his chest and let loose the tears that have been building up from holding in this secret of seeing my own death. I can't handle this burden. I'm too young for this. Sure, I hunt ghosts and I talk to spirits like it's no big deal, but this is messing with my plans for my life. It wasn't an older version of myself I saw battered and bleeding, it was me—now.

How do I share this news?

Jason gently shakes me. "Kendall. Talk to me, damnit."

He moves his thumbs under my eyes to wipe away the salty tears. There's such love and care in his face that I know I have to come clean. It's the right thing to do.

I take a deep breath to steady my nerves. "Jason, I need to tell you something."

His hands return to my shoulders and knead them to show me he's listening. "You know you can tell me anything."

I smirk slightly, aware there's a part of him that's still quite skeptical about my abilities. "It's kind of . . . out there."

Leaning in, Jason kisses me quickly on the lips and grins. "I'm used to your 'out there' stories, K."

Another cleansing breath. "I've had a really scary vision."

"About what? Us?"

The vision of almost kissing the brown-eyed guy is too fresh. I have to let that one soak in a little more before I try to interpret that. "No. About me."

"What about you?"

"Jason, I've . . ." *Steady, girl.* "I've visualized my own death."

He sits back into the pillows and huffs out a long breath. "We're all going to die one day, Kendall. So what?"

"No, like . . . soon."

"What do you mean?"

I explain the vision to him in detail, just as I dreamed it two months ago. My emotions boil over as I'm finally able to share this with someone else. "And it ended with me . . . dead."

Jason's usually tan face turns white as the clichéd sheet and I can see the alpha wolf in him begin to emerge, teeth bared and eyes determined. "I won't let it happen."

Shaking my head, I say, "If it's my future, there's nothing you can do about it."

"Like hell there isn't! I'll do everything in my power to protect you."

"You can't."

His lips flatten. "Try stopping me."

Awww . . . how sweet is he? I launch myself at him and hug tightly. "I love you so much, Jason."

"I love you too, Kendall," he says into my hair. "I won't let that vision come true. I just won't."

I squeeze my eyes shut, trapping the tears that so want to escape. I bask in the shelter of Jason's love and protection . . . at least momentarily. The light on the nightstand flickers and I know that Emily is near. When I open my eyes, she's watching me and shaking her head.

"You shouldn't have told him . . ."

I ignore her interference and she fades away as fast as she appeared.

Jason pushes me back slightly and cocks an eyebrow toward the light. "Your invisible friend?"

I nod. "She didn't want me telling anyone."

"I'm not just anyone, Kendall. And I will protect you no matter what. I don't want you going anywhere without me, or even driving over the speed limit."

Laughing, I say, "It doesn't happen in a car."

"You don't know that!"

"Yeah, I do. It happens inside. In a house. Near some stairs."

"Then I don't want you doing any investigations. I'm serious. You never know what you'll encounter that might want to make this vision a reality."

"Oh, please. I can totally still drive. And I'm not giving up ghost hunting. It's my calling and there are too many families out there that need my help. Like Mayor Shy. Can you believe the mayor wants us to investigate her house?"

"You're not to do it without me," he says firmly.

"Whatever."

"It's not whatever, K. I'm serious."

"So am I. I'll be as careful as I always am. I just had to tell you what's been eating at me so you'll understand."

Jason kisses my forehead and whispers his love to me. "I'll always protect you, Kendall. I'll be damned if I'll let anything hurt you."

As we hug, I'm somewhat relieved to have shared this with someone. Saying it out loud makes it sound less possible. And as Loreen always says to me, the future truly is up to us.

I just have to see where mine takes me.

CHAPTER THREE

"CAN WE CLOSE THE SUMMERFIELD CASE?" Becca asks. She, Celia, Taylor, and I are all spread out in my room going through our case files. "Didn't we debunk everything?"

"I don't remember that one," I say, my mind in ten thousand other locations at the moment.

"Sure you do, Kendall," Taylor says. She reaches a perfectly manicured hand across the carpet to snag the folder from Becca. "This was the one where that nice lady named Delia said she smelled cigarette smoke all around her house and thought she recognized the brand of smokes and that it was her deceased mother trying to reach out to her."

I nod my head. "Riiiiiight. But it was really her niece sneaking out onto the roof every night and smoking a butt."

Celia snickers. "I love it when we solve a case like that. Everyone all of a sudden thinks a house is haunted when anything out of the ordinary happens, but sometimes it's just possessed by the living."

Taylor scrunches up her pretty face. "I think it's sad when

people call us over because they're so lonely and want someone to talk to. *Très misérable.*"

Becca adjusts her nose stud with her index finger. "There are a lot of lost people out there, Tay." She stares forward with a knowledge of how true that statement is. Becca used to be popular and a beauty queen until her grandmother passed away and Becca felt responsible for it. She wasn't, of course, but she's not the same person she used to be because of what she went through when she lost her grandmother. Her Goth look is testament to that. Although the only person I've loved and lost is my Grandma Ethel, I've learned through my ghost hunting that each and every person in this world deals with death differently. Becca's taken it further than most with her complete transformation. Still, she's one of my best friends and one of the nicest people I know.

"Remember that guy who showed us his butterfly collection?" Celia remarks as she fiddles with her K-II meter. "We sat there for what seemed like hours listening to how they go from egg to larva to pupa to butterfly . . . like I don't know that."

Celia's quite the go-to gal when it comes to all things science, so I can feel her pain as she reminisces about the visit with one Mr. Norbert Bates of Cokesbury Lane in Radisson.

"Come on, Cel," I say, empathizing with Mr. Bates. "The old guy had no one to talk to and invented the ghost in his basement so we'd come over and chat with him."

"For an hour?" Celia responds.

"That's what the Internet is for, dude," Becca quips, and I laugh.

"Thank God we had Father Massimo with us," Taylor says. Then she adds, "No pun intended."

Mentors like Loreen and Father Mass are good "body-guards" for us as well. We try not to go into any strange person's house (too many local crackpots) without adult supervision. Not that we're irresponsible or anything like that. It just pays to have an adult with us to run interference or get us out of a weird sitch . . . like the butterfly show with Mr. Bates.

Celia pulls her laptop over between the two of us and scrolls through the requests from Ghosthuntress.com. Our website gets tons of hits from people looking for help with whatever might be haunting them. Word about our little group has certainly spread like wildfire around these parts. Lately, though, the requests seem to be getting stranger and stranger.

Celia jabs her fingers into her thick black hair and scratches at her head. "I don't know which one we should take next. There's a case of a floating head seen by a seventy-year-old man in his barn in Triple Creek—which is like four hours south of here—and then there's the couple who claim a demon lives in the central A/C in their house."

I hold up my hands. "No demonic cases. We're not demon-ologists and don't need to get caught up in that at all."

Becca agrees. "Damn straight. I'm not messing with that shit."

"None of us are," Celia remarks and continues to scroll through the e-mails. "God, aren't *any* of these requests local? I swear, we're spending too much in gas money getting to and from these investigations."

"Not like we're getting reimbursed for our costs."

I remind them, "No legitimate ghost-hunting group charges for their services."

"I know," Becca says. "Sometimes I wish we could, though. This traveling around is getting tough on the old teenage budget."

Taylor frowns again. "And I hardly get any time alone with Ryan these days. He's starting to think I like ghost hunting more than dating him."

I sigh long and hard, moving my hair with the heated breath. "I know how that is."

Boys. If you're not giving them one hundred percent of your attention and time, they get so needy. Not that I wouldn't like to spend more time with Jason. Since basketball season is in full swing for Radisson High School, we really need a local case to work on that will keep us from traveling and perhaps walking into a messed-up situation with someone who lives far away and that we don't know at all.

This is a good time to tell them about my convo with Mayor Shy. "If we want a local case, I've got one for us. Just talked to the owner yesterday."

"What is it?" Celia asks with her eyebrow raised. She's always poised to act on my ideas.

"It's the mayor's house."

"Awesome," Becca says.

Celia starts scribbling in her notebook. "What is she experiencing?"

I recount the history of my interaction with Donn Shy: "Well, I told you, Mayor Shy has been coming into Divining Woman for me to do tarot readings for her? She's been complaining to Loreen about all of these back problems—she doesn't know where they've come from."

Celia keeps writing in her notebook. "What are the symptoms?"

"Body ache, headaches, severe back pain," I tell her. "Her masseuse hasn't been able to pinpoint or solve the problems. Her doctor can't find anything like a break or strain or pinched nerve on the X-rays. A chiropractor was no help, and acupuncture isn't working."

"What can we do about someone's back problems?" Becca asks.

"It's not so much the back pain," I explain. "She and I have been working on the pressure points with attunement-activation healing sessions."

"That thing you've been learning to do with the pitchforks?" Becca asks.

"Tuning forks. Not pitchforks . . . geesh!" I say with a laugh. "Attunement-energy healing uses the sounds and vibrations from the tuning forks to adjust whatever maladies ail you." Damn, I'm talking like a fifty-year-old all of a sudden.

"I'm with Becca," Taylor interjects. "What does her back problem have to do with an investigation?"

"There's something haunting the mayor's mansion and I think it's affecting her physically," I say.

Taylor's eyes grow wide with excitement. "Shut *up!*"

I tell my friends about the woman I saw in the window and how I just *feel* like something is messing with Mayor Shy in a way I can't explain unless we can get into the house for a full investigation. "I think we need both Loreen and Father Mass with us because deep down, I'd say we need all the help we can get with this case. The woman in the window didn't look like she wanted to leave anytime soon."

"We can't force a spirit out if it doesn't want to go," Celia says.

"No, you're right. We can, however, connect with her, and I'll try to explain that she's harming the living that are still there."

"You think Mayor Shy would be up to an investigation?" Taylor asks. "I've always wanted to see the inside of that gorgeous house. I mean, I've never been inside, but it seems *très* chic and I bet I could take some awesome pictures of the inside and maybe submit them to a Southern-living type magazine."

"She's definitely on board."

Celia wets her bottom lip and I can see she's excited by the prospect of getting to explore one of Radisson's oldest and most historic dwellings. "I'll start doing the research on it. You"—she looks directly at me—"set it up and then we'll get to work."

"I'll confirm with her," I say, happy to help out.

Excellent. A local ghost hunt that will keep the boyfriends happy because they can spend more time with us and the parents pleased because we won't be traveling too far away. And my own mind can—hopefully—relax more, knowing I'll be close to home in case this doomed destiny hits.

"How does that feel?"

Mayor Donn Shy reaches around and rubs her left shoulder, which I've been working on for the last twenty minutes with the tuning-fork attunement-activation healing. "It tingles."

I smile. "That's all part of the energy working around you." I ting the tuning forks together and roll them in the air around each other, stirring up the energy field surrounding the mayor. I continue to ting and twirl the forks as I move around her, hoping to heal the pain in her shoulders and back. "Just keep breathing."

Loreen peeks through the velvet curtain and winks at me. "Everything okay back here?"

Mayor Shy smiles a vibrant white grin. "You've got an amazing gal here, Loreen."

"Thanks," I say, feeling the blush splash my face. "I have a good client here."

I notice that Loreen is wearing a soft cream-colored blouse and freshly ironed khaki slacks instead of her usual jeans and silly-saying T-shirt. Her curls are brushed neatly into place around her face, and her lips shimmer slightly with a pale pink gloss.

"Hot date?" I ask, only half kidding. I've never seen her dressed up like this before.

Her own blush gives her away. "I was, um, going to leave early tonight if you don't mind locking up, Kendall."

The mayor and I exchange knowing glances.

"You seriously have a date!" I exclaim. An image appears to me of Loreen sitting at a nice restaurant at a candlelit table holding hands with . . .

"Oh my God! You're going out with Father Massimo?" How cool is that! I totally saw *that* hookup coming.

Loreen turns twelve shades of crimson—if that's even possible—and drops the curtain between us. I excuse myself as the mayor chuckles at our escapades.

"Loreen! That is awesome!" I say as I come behind the curtain.

She waves me off. "Now, don't make a big deal out of it, Kendall."

My cheesy grin is too wide to hide. "Yeah, I will. I knew you two had something brewing. I could feel it a couple of months ago."

"Well, we have been seeing each other for coffee here and there, nothing serious."

"Not yet," I say with an assurance like no other reading I've done before. I've seen the two of them together in my mind's eye, but now I'm completely one hundred percent sure that they are each other's soul mates. "And to think . . . *I* brought you together."

"Enough," Loreen says with a laugh. "It's only dinner at the Kirby Pines."

"Hmm . . . every kiss begins with *k*," I say, paraphrasingthe advertisement for Kay Jewelers. The Kirby Pines is a fancy restaurant on the outskirts of Radisson where kids go on prom dates and such and where parents go to celebrate big occasions. Father Mass must really be trying to impress Loreen. I think it's adorable.

"Kendall." She moans and rolls her eyes. "Lock up when you're done."

"Yes, ma'am," I say in an exaggerated Southern drawl.

When the store door closes behind my mentor, I return to my customer. "So sorry about that, Mayor Shy, but I couldn't *not* comment on all of that."

"Sweetie, call me Donn," she says with a kind smile. "I think it's wonderful that Loreen's getting out. She's been a loner for as long as I've been in town. That hot priest is sure to show her a good time."

Ewww . . . while I'm happy to see Loreen and Father Mass hooking up, I don't want to *think* about them hooking up. Too. Much. Information.

I pick up the Mercury tuning fork and clutch it to me. "They've both been really supportive of me since I moved here and awakened to my psychic abilities. I just want them both to be happy."

Donn reaches out a thin, tanned hand and clasps it around my wrist. "You're a special girl, Kendall."

I swallow the lump in my throat and get back to work on my client. "Thanks, Donn."

For the next fifteen minutes, I use the Mercury tuning fork to ground Donn's energy surrounding her. There's a whole set of larger tuning forks that Loreen bought for me that are aligned to each of the planets. The Earth gets so much of its energies from sister planets, the sun, and the moon.

"What's the large tuning fork for?" Donn asks as I wave it in front of her face.

"Mercury is in retrograde right now," I explain. "That means that communication can be disrupted. You're not supposed to make any big decisions or sign anything important. A lot of times computers get all kerflukey, and e-mail tends not to work while Mercury's in retrograde."

"You know your stuff, Kendall."

"I try. I feel like I read as many books on being psychic and on energy healing as I do schoolbooks."

"It shows."

I strike the large fork on the meaty part of my palm and then touch the end of it to Donn's left shoulder until I no longer feel the vibration from it. The longer it vibrates, the more that spot on the body needs energy. Donn's shoulder certainly needed the help.

"Ooo . . . that feels wonderful," she says in a long sigh.

As I finish up the healing session, I figure now's as good a time as any to mention that the team is willing to investigate the mayor's mansion.

"Mayor, er, I mean, Donn, so I talked to my team about investigating your house?"

She opens her eyes. "Are they interested?"

I lick my lips and forge ahead. "And how. You said the other day that your house was haunted. Is that just a thing you say to visitors in town because of the Civil War history? Or have you ever had anything weird happen while you've been living there?"

Donn adjusts her small wire-rimmed glasses on the bridge of her nose. I can see the wheels of thought turning in her head as she carefully considers the question. After a moment, she flattens her thin lips together. "I believe my Mayer is still around me. He died so quickly when the heart attack took him. I don't know if he had time to know what was happening to him."

"They—the *they* that are experts in everything—say we never fully comprehend what's occurring when we pass on. Not that I'd know or anything, but that's just what I've come across in my studies."

"I'm sure my Mayer found his way to heaven. It's just that I like to think that he checks in with me every now and then to make sure I'm doing okay and not futzing around with any of the city ordinances he put into place." She laughs deep down in her chest and I join in. I don't sense her husband anywhere near at the present time. Though who am I to say he's not around her at other times?

Bravely, I ask, "Well, when we come in to investigate, I can get a sense psychically of what's going on, if anything. You know, we could take some pictures, do some recordings to see if we capture anything on the digital voice recorders . . . maybe Mayer has a message for you?"

"Right! Like on those ghost-hunting shows on television? I love watching those."

Nodding, I say, "That's what my group does. We've investigated a ton of places and gotten a lot of evidence." I want to ask her about the woman behind the curtain. However, it seems that even the mayor doesn't know about the extra guest in her house. "You never know if there are other spirits present, considering how old and historic your house is."

Donn rotates her left shoulder and lets out a contented sigh. My nose itches a bit with my heightened psychic abilities, and I know that she's feeling much better. The attunement-activation healing session has worked on her.

"Next weekend would be perfect then, if it works with you gals," Donn says. "The new housekeeper is starting on Monday, so the manor's in a little disarray. The last woman left me so suddenly and created a mess in her wake."

I furrow my brow. "Why did she leave?"

The mayor shrugs as she reaches for her purse. "Who knows? Tallulah was always a strange one, tripping all the time and breaking things. It's a good thing she quit before I fired her. I couldn't afford to lose any more china."

I breathe deeply and center my thoughts on what Mayor Shy is relaying to me. I see Tallulah, an older woman with curly red hair pinned back behind her ears. She's dusting the china cabinet at the mayor's mansion when suddenly dishes begin flying off the shelf onto the floor. Tallulah screams and backs away from the shattering glass. Someone else is making this happen. The housekeeper grabs rosaries out of her hip pocket and closes her eyes in prayer. The woman doesn't believe in ghosts or spirits and soon goes about her work again, only to be tripped on her way to the kitchen. The entity that resides in the mayor's mansion does not like Tallulah. I know that for a fact and can sense it clear as a bell. But I don't feel like this is something I can share with the mayor until I get a handle on exactly who this spirit is.

One thing's obivious: she's not a happy ghost.

But then again, a lot of the ones I encounter aren't. Mostly they're scared, confused, misinformed, or just unaware of their own circumstances. Celia said she's researching the manor and its history, and we'll get on it to see what we're up against.

"I'll gather the team and we'll be there next Saturday night."

Donn pats me on the shoulder. "Sounds perfect. Maybe I'll hang around with you for the fun."

Fun? I don't think so. We'll see . . .

Donn reaches into her purse and extracts thirty dollars for me.

"The session's only twenty," I say.

"A tip," she says with a friendly smile.

"Thanks, Mayor Shy. I mean, Donn."

"You're a miracle worker, Kendall. I haven't felt this good in weeks. Whatever it was you did worked like a charm. I look forward to welcoming you and your friends."

I take the cash and grin my thanks.

The over-the-door bell rings out as the mayor exits the store. I follow behind her and click shut the dead bolt. I place the cash in the register and then lock it as well.

I check my BlackBerry to find several text messages from Jason.

> Thinking of u!

> Everything ok?

> Don't do anything ghostly w/out me.

> Why haven't u answered me??? R u ok?

> Call me!

Awww . . . he's so adorable, worrying about me like this. No one could ask for a better boyfriend.

As I'm speed-dialing Jason, I'm suddenly struck with the most horrendous nausea and stomach cramps. I drop my BlackBerry on the hardwood floor as I double over in excruciating pain. My cell phone hits hard and breaks apart into three pieces; the battery and SIM card skitter out and scatter. I can't worry about the electronics at this moment or what might have happened to the call to Jason. All I know is I feel like someone has stabbed me in the gut with a large chef's knife. Like the one Mom keeps next to the stove for chopping and cutting. A searing throb of ache cripples me, warning me of things to come. This isn't someone else's injury I'm feeling. It's not empathy or reliving a past event. This is clearly a premonition. A physical demonstration to illustrate the stunning image of my own end.

"No . . ." I call out to no one as the tears trickle out of the corners of my eyes. "I won't let this happen. I won't think about it." I have no idea who I'm talking to, whether it's Emily who might be listening or God himself.

I breathe through the anguish, not giving in to the prospect that lies ahead of me. By recognizing the possibility, I only encourage these visions to manifest in reality.

I gather the pieces of my phone and push out of Divining Woman, barely remembering to lock the back door behind me. Once I'm outside in the waning daylight hours, my breathing begins to settle. With shaky hands, I put the cellular device back together. Immediately, Jason's number appears on the LED.

"Hey," I say, trying to steady my inhalation. "What's up?" Taking the casual approach so as not to give in to what just happened.

"Are you all right, Kendall?" Jason asks furiously. "I've been worried sick about you!"

"I've been at work."

"You could have texted me!"

"I was with a customer."

"Kendall, you can't just drop a shit bomb like you did and not expect me to worry about you constantly. I'm not wound that way."

"I'm fine, Jase. Really I am."

I hate lying to him, but there's no reason to upset him further until I find out what's going on. For some reason, my senses are saying that everything centers around whatever it is that was glaring at me in Mayor Shy's house. Until I can get to the bottom of that, I'll have to keep up with my daily routine and keep keeping on.

I will *not* manifest this impending tragedy.

"Where are you?" he asks. "I'm coming to get you."

"No worries. I've got my car." However, my hand trembles as I reach to place the key in the car door. "I'll be home in five minutes."

"I'll be there when you get there." Then he clicks off the phone without saying goodbye.

I'm not offended. I know he's just concerned.

Sitting behind the wheel of the Fit, I take a deep gulp of air and then slowly release it. A crank and a shift into reverse and then into first, and I'm on my way down Main Street to my house. After Jason leaves tonight, I'm going to have a long convo with Emily to get to the bottom of all this.

CHAPTER FOUR

I HATE IT WHEN A GHOST COPS AN ATTITUDE with you.

"Emily, why won't you just answer my questions?"

"Because you ask questions that I can't answer."

"Can't . . . or won't?" I toss my pillow at Emily, who's sitting in my rocker with Sonoma the bear. I can see him through her body as she makes the chair move back and forth somehow. Of course the pillow doesn't faze her. She's dead.

"We've had this conversation before, Kendall."

"And we'll keep having it until you give me some answers. Come on, Emily. You're my spirit guide. Do some frickin' guiding here, would you?"

"I don't know what more I can do. I'm here for you as much as I can be."

I grind my top teeth against the bottom ones. Frustration boils under my skin. Father Mass's Sunday sermon this morning was on the topic of patience, but I have none at the moment. "Let's take this from the top again," I say with a bit of sarcasm icing my speech. "I have a dream where you're in a burning vehicle, pregnant, with a dead boyfriend behind the wheel. Then the image shifts into me in a heap on the floor, bleeding to death internally. What 'more' you can do for me is interpret this dream in more detail than saying that I saw your past and my future."

"I can't do that . . ."

I throw my hands up in the air. "Again with the can't. Is there some code of the undead that you're in jeopardy of breaking?

"Now Kendall . . ."

"Don't!" I hold my hand up in front of me toward the spirit of the woman who died too young. She could be my college-age sister from how she looks, except for the morbid hospital gown she's apparently doomed to wear for all of eternity. I never realized I could be so perturbed at someone who doesn't really exist. "Don't 'Kendall' me like you're Sarah Moorehead. Only she can talk to me like that. I want some answers and I want them now."

Emily's head slumps, her long brown hair falling into her pale face. She plays with one of the ties on her hospital gown, rolling it between her thumb and forefinger.

"There are certain things we know on this side that simply can't be shared with the living. Things you have to learn on your own. Or at the right time."

I blow out an annoyed gust of air. "Are you telling me that I have to *die* to know the truth about you? About my own future?"

She shakes her head.

I stand and begin pacing between my bed and dresser. Aggravation burns in my chest like nasty heartburn from too many jalapeños on my movie nachos. "You're pissing me off, Emily. Who was the guy that died in the car with you and why isn't he here haunting me as well?"

"Kendall . . . I . . ."

"I know. You can't tell me." I head for the bedroom door. My stomach growls at the smell of Mom's homemade spaghetti that's wafting up from the kitchen. The piquant smell of onions, pepperonis, and fresh tomatoes does little to soothe my annoyance. I spin back around only to find Emily right behind me, her hand on my shoulder. I feel nothing, though. Her touch is as much a phantom as the mystery that surrounds her.

"You tell me you're here to help me. You tell me you're here to guide me. You tell me you've been with me my whole life. You tell me that you care about me. You tell me all of this crap and bullshit, Emily. It means nothing if you won't help me through this." I poke my index finger into my chest for emphasis. "I'm scared, Emily. Scared out of my wits. Don't you understand that?"

Her beautiful face falls into a heartbreaking frown. I think if she were able to cry, she would.

"All I can tell you, Kendall, is that I love you, but there are limits to what I can do for you."

I can't hide my disdain and she sees it. I open my door and slam it shut between us.

If Emily won't tell me the truth about her former life and how it affects me, I know who can get to the bottom of it.

With her smarts and determination, Celia Nichols could find a lost contact lens in an Olympic-size pool.

The hell with conversing with a ghost. A living soul will solve this.

On Tuesday, The lunchroom at RHS is rollicking with the sounds of Becca's fresh Trance groove, the hubbub of the cheerleaders selling tickets to the end-of-winter dance, and a short-lived rumble over God knows what between Dragon—Becca's boyfriend—and Marcus Stafford.

I set my tray down next to Taylor, who eyeballs my macaroni and cheese.

"I *knew* I should have gotten that instead of the meat loaf," she says with a pout.

"Have some of mine."

She beams at me and picks up her fork to dig in.

Across the table, Celia looks like she hasn't slept since we talked on Sunday night. When I asked her for help on researching Emily, I had no idea she'd turn it into her own personal season of *CSI*. Her hair is a mess, she has slight dark circles under her eyes, and she's on her second iced coffee of the day.

"Dude, you look like crap," I say, knowing she won't take it as a personal affront.

Celia lifts her dark eyes at me momentarily and then shifts

them back to the stack of papers in front of her. Her laptop is off to the side, and I can see several browser windows opened.

"No time for sleep. Too much to even tell you right now."

Clay Price, her boyfriend, plops down and slides a grilled cheese and bacon in front of her. He loops his long arm around the back of her chair and glances over her shoulder without Celia even blinking. "What's this secretive research project you've got her working on, K?"

"It's not a secret, Clay," she corrects him. "It's my new obsession to find these answers for Kendall."

"Such as?" Taylor asks, uncharacteristically talking with her mouth full. I better dig into my mac 'n' cheese before she Hoovers it all down.

Fisting a handful of papers, Celia looks at Taylor, Clay, and then me, her eyes wide. "You wouldn't believe what-all I've been doing. I've been Googling the hell out of every published police report for the last twenty years from San Francisco to Bar Harbor, Maine."

Taylor's fork stops midair. "You can do that?"

"Oh, yeah," Celia says with a sly smile. "My cousin Paul Nichols is with the GBI and he's been helping me out."

"GBI?" I ask.

"Georgia Bureau of Investigations," Celia and Clay say in unison.

"Oh." Who knew? "What's he been helping out with?"

Celia tugs out the drawings that she and I have done of Emily. Celia's a whiz with a set of colored pencils and was able to capture Emily's image based on my description. "I faxed these to Paul and asked him to run it through the national databases."

I'm riveted. "Of what?"

"Missing persons. Jane Does. Things like that. I told him to be looking for a DOA from a car wreck at any hospital."

"And don't forget that she was pregnant. There has to be a record of the child's death as well."

"Why do you assume *l'enfant* died too?" Taylor asks with such clarity.

I cock my head to the side. "I never assumed that the baby lived. You've got a point, Taylor."

"Thanks!" She reaches her fork over. "Does that afford me more of your mac 'n' cheese?"

Jason appears behind us and drops a five spot on the table. "Go get your own, Tay."

She pockets the Lincoln and continues to dive into my rather large portion.

"Hey, babe," he says, leaning down to kiss my cheek. He fist bumps Clay across the table before sitting next to me. "Whatch'all doing?"

"Celia's trying to figure out who Emily *truly* is . . . or was."

Jason shakes his head. "I tell you, I wish she'd just leave you alone most of the time. Did Kendall tell y'all what Emily did to me?"

"What?" Clay asks.

I smack Jason hard on the arm, not wanting him to share

our hot and heavy make-out session that ended with Emily giving him a wedgie. I'd be mortified if everyone knew that. "Never mind. Let Celia concentrate."

She points her pen in my direction. "Do you have any inkling of where this car accident occurred?"

I screw my mouth up. "Not really. Just that it was raining and there was a bad wreck and the car caught fire and the guy driving died."

"God, that would be half the battle in solving this mystery," Celia says. She lets out a long breath of air and moves her hand through her long bangs. "Of course, it would be a whole hell of a lot easier if Emily would just *tell* you herself."

After finally taking a taste of my own lunch, I swallow the creaminess and say, "Emily insists that I not pursue it."

"You'd think with your psychic abilities, you could figure some of this out on your own," Taylor adds.

No truer statement has ever been made.

The bell rings, ending our lunch period, so we all scoop and cram our food, gather our books, and head out to our next classes. Jason gives me a quick kiss and promises to text me, telling me to be careful. Like what's going to happen to me at school?

Taylor runs off to catch up with her boyfriend, Ryan. They're too cute. I can totally see them together forever, living in a house with a white picket fence and having a dog, a cat, and 2.3 children.

As I walk toward calculus class, I wonder about poor Emily's child. Did it live? If so, whatever became of him or her? Was the baby adopted? Did it grow up in an orphanage? Do we even still have orphanages in America?

Celia breezes by me, her backpack bulging with her computer and research material. "Let me know if you have any other visions or anything. My cousin Paul is supposed to call me tonight."

I give her the thumb's-up sign and walk into my classroom only to hear the teacher say, "Get settled as quickly as you can. We're having a pop quiz."

The groans and moans of thirty students echo throughout the room.

I can't worry about Emily right now. I've got vectors to battle.

Twenty-two minutes into the quiz, my eyes start blurring over at the figures on the paper in front of me. I can no longer make out the questions, even though I blink wicked hard to try to focus. No matter how hard I squint, I can't see any of the test questions. Great . . . how do I explain *this* to the teacher?

A hazy fog fills my vision and then clears as quickly as it came.

I see Emily. She's trapped in the burning car, one hand on her distended stomach and the other pounding on the passenger-side window. I can't do anything to help her or get to her. But I do get a look at the car. It's a white Monte Carlo from, like, the mid-1980s. I've seen old cars like that around Radisson because their owners are too frugal to invest in a newer hybrid or what have you. In my mind's eye, I move around to the back of the car for a look at the license plate.

I concentrate hard on the image.

A red barn.

Birds.

A sailboat in the upper right-hand corner.

America's Dairyland comes into view.

Wisconsin. It's a Wisconsin plate.

And I see the tag plain as day.

Dark red letters: WKA-111.

Immediately, I'm jolted out of my haze. Forgetting my pop quiz, I reach for my cell phone and text Celia:

>We have our break.

Chapter Five

THAT NIGHT, MY DREAMS ARE FRAUGHT with myriad disturbing images that I have no control over. Emily's car wreck. Emily going into labor. Emily's boyfriend slumped over the steering wheel while the car crackles and sizzles away under the intense fiery blaze. My mother with Emily. What? My *mother* with Emily? WTF? Now I'm just going insane. Then Jason is there telling me to be careful, begging, in fact.

Suddenly, people surround me on my left and my right with a chant that everything will be okay. It will? What isn't okay, that they have to tell me that? And then there's a guy there. Not Jason . . . someone else. He looks like he might be my age or maybe a year older. Who even knows in dreams? He's got delicious chocolate brown eyes, jet-black eyebrows, and longish, shaggy black hair that's actually peppered with grays around his temples. Grays? At our age? There's something about him, though. A knowingness that we're part of each other's lives. Or will be. He's familiar, yet not. He calls out to me with a deep voice I don't recognize. Is this someone who's coming into my life? Or merely a figment of my imagination? Or is he another spirit guide, like Emily?

The images shift quickly, thoroughly erasing Hershey Eyes and flashing back to me lying on the floor, clutching my side in excruciating pain, knowing without a doubt that I'm bleeding to death internally. *Stop it! Someone help me!* I scream out though no words leave my lips. The pain is frenzied and intense, like thousands of fire ants crawling all over my body. Not that that's ever happened to me, but Celia recently told me a story about when she was nine years old and visited her cousin's farm and sat in a pile of them. They had to strip off her clothes and spray her down with the hose to get the stinging creatures off her. Am I merely empathizing with that long-ago story or is this really happening to me?

Death permeates my nostrils as spirits rise from the ground to surround me. They call out to me and welcome me to their ranks. Ghostly fingers curl around my limbs, tugging and pulling and coaxing. But I won't go! I'm too young to die. Someone do something!

I wake up screaming, tangled in the sheets like they're octopus tentacles. Sweat dots my upper lip and also trickles down the back of my neck, drenching my hair into frizzy curls that will need massive products to calm them down. I hear panting like there's an exhausted dog in the room, but then I realize the windedness is coming from me.

"Mom!" I cry out, wanting nothing but to be held close in her arms with her whispering words of love and comfort to me.

Emily sits quietly in the rocker, tipping it back and forth like she enjoys doing. She's humming a soft, sweet melody, something reminiscent of a lullaby. The tune seems familiar to me, only not.

"Shhh . . . Kendall . . . close your eyes . . ."

"But the dreams. The visions. The nightmares," I say in a gasping whisper.

"Go back to sleep."

"I can't." The words leave me in nearly a whimper.

I glance over at the clock, which reads some ungodly hour. Surely my parents are sound asleep and unaware of my troubles. Part of me wants to walk down the hall and crawl into bed with them, like I used to do when I was little and had a stomachache. I'm too old to do that, though, and the worry over the truth of what's going on with me would no doubt disturb my mom and dad no end.

"I don't want these dreams anymore."

"I'm watching over you, Kendall. Just like I always have. Even when you couldn't see me."

Somehow these words soothe me enough to lull me back into a dreamless sleep, the gently hummed lullaby serenading me.

The peace is short-lived though.

Wednesday morning my senses are at a Homeland Security threat level of red.

On the way into the bathroom, I trip over Kaitlin's soccer shoes and go sprawling forward in the most spasmodic way.

The cast-iron claw-foot tub anchored to the bathroom floor seems to be coming toward me at a tremendous velocity. I cringe as I do a tuck and roll like I learned in gym class in elementary school. A sigh rushes out of my chest as I come this close to cracking my skull open on the base of the tub.

Mom peeks her head into the bathroom as I lie on the rug catching my breath. "Kendall, what *are* you doing?"

Surviving? Avoiding my death? Losing my mind?

"I tripped on Kaitlin's farging shoes in the middle of the floor."

Mom tsk-tsks me. "Such language, dear." Then she calls out, "Kaitlin! What have I told you about leaving your soccer equipment all over the place?"

After my shower, even the sounds of Snap, Crackle, and Pop in my cereal bowl skeeve me out. Is everything out to get me? Is there such a thing as death by Krispies?

Dad reaches over and touches my arm. I jump in my seat like I've been electrocuted.

"Nervous much?" he says with a sweet laugh.

"Oh, sorry. I was just, um, thinking about school stuff."

"I asked if you're going to Loreen's after school today."

Am I? Do I even want to? I mostly want to come back home, strap myself into my bed, and ride out this wave of fear of the unknown.

"I'll probably go over to Celia's," I finally eke out. "We're working on a project together." There, that sounds legit. Parents always want to hear that their kids are concentrating on school stuff. I dare not tell them what's possibly on the horizon for me. If I did, I'd be locked in the attic and homeschooled until I was through my graduate degree.

"Sounds good, kiddo." Dad gets up, puts his coffee mug in the sink, and then bends down to kiss me on the forehead. "Have a great day at school."

"Sure thing, Dad."

Can I really, though?

Thursday after school, Celia texts me to come over to her house. I push aside my assignment for calculus—which I'm starting to loathe—and tromp across the backyard, trying not to step on anything poisonous that's out to get me.

Paranoid much?

I slip through the gate and over the small road to the Nicholses's mansion. Alice, their housekeeper, greets me at the door, as does Seamus, Celia's snarly yet lovable bulldog. He leads me up the stairs to her room as if I've never been here before.

"Dude! Get in here," Celia shouts when she hears me coming.

"What's up?"

"That plate number you came up with gave us a hit."

"Gave who a hit?"

Proudly, Celia reports, "My cousin Paul, with the GBI, found a record from 1992 in Wisconsin. The car was registered to an E. J. Faulkner."

"*E* . . . as in *Emily!*"

"Paul's checking it. But it looks like we've at least got a last name for her," Celia reports.

"Emily Faulkner." I let the name trip over my lips as well as slosh around in my head for a bit. "That's great, but it doesn't put me anywhere closer to knowing about her past or her baby or anything." I slump down onto Celia's bed and stare up at the ceiling.

"I thought of that," Celia says, confident as ever. "I asked Paul to run the name through the national database of missing persons. Give him some time, Kendall, he'll find our ghost."

I've found her, though. Emily is standing next to me.

"Why are you doing this, Kendall?"

"Doing what, Emily? Finding out who you really are?" I ask out loud.

Celia turns her head in my direction. "Is she here with us?"

"Isn't it enough that I'm here to help you contact other spirits and work through your own problems? Why do you have to dig up my past?"

"Because, Emily Faulkner," I say with emphasis, "you told me that *my* future was tied to *your* past. I think that's a pretty important sticking point."

"Come on, Emily." Celia looks around as if she can see the ghost. "Why don't you save my cousin and me valuable time and just dish all the info to Kendall now?"

Emily glares at me.

"She says it doesn't work that way," I relay. Then I turn back to Emily. "Stubborn."

"Look, Kendall. We'll get the information in due time. Between Googling and my cousin's efforts at the GBI, we'll find out who Emily really is."

"And then what?"

Can Emily stop my future from happening? Can I? What good is any of this doing?

"Then you can pass her into the light where she belongs," Celia says. "That's what all of this is about. Working with the earthbound spirits that only you can connect with."

"Right...helping the spirits," I mutter. I've been so wrapped up in my own dreams and visions that I've forgotten the whole goal of my team of ghost huntresses. It's not about me. Not. About. Me. It's not about what's in it for me. It's about helping the confused entities resolve whatever is troubling them enough to keep them from their eternal peace. I totally have to get over myself and quit wallowing around in self-pity because of some stupid dreams that may or may not come to be.

I speak to Emily. "I know you're here to help me and teach me how to use my abilities to assist the living and the deceased. If you don't want to tell me who you really are and what your past is all about, that's fine. I've got plenty of other spirits who need my help. If you're around to whisper clues into my ear like you've done in the past, that's awesome, but I won't be held prisoner by fear or visions or ... whatever."

"What visions?" Celia asks.

"Just stuff."

"Have it your way, Kendall ..."

Emily gently fades away, and a sense of overwhelming sadness coats me. I can't worry about Emily anymore. She's a grown woman. Well . . . she was until she died.

"Something you haven't told me?" Celia seems crushed that I'd hide anything from her. It's not that I'm being deceitful. I just don't want *another* person obsessed with worry about me. Jason's got that in the bag.

I fib slightly—though is withholding information really lying? Semantics, I know. "I told you all about seeing Emily die. I'm going to step back and let you work on that. If you and your cousin find anything out about her, that's great. If not, I'm not going to worry about it. We've got an investigation at Mayor Shy's house this weekend, and I need to get a handle on calculus." I'm supposed to be working on this side paper about Zeno, a Greek philosopher who is known for Zeno's paradox. What a narcissist, naming some stupid calculus theory after yourself!

Celia salutes me like a good soldier and dives back to her computer. "Then, if you're telling me you're okay, I won't follow you around school anymore with the EMF detector."

"What the—" I say, sitting up and shaking my head in disbelief. "Please tell me you're joking."

"Hello! Have you just met me?"

Only Celia Nichols would take to EMFing someone she thought was in trouble. I swat at her for good measure. "Let's call Taylor and Becca over and we can go through the details of Saturday night's investigation."

"Sounds perfect." Celia whips out a set of blueprints from underneath her desk. "These are the schematics of the mayor's mansion. I thought they'd come in useful for us when we're setting up base camp and our equipment."

I'm almost speechless. "Where on God's green earth did you get the blueprints?"

She shrugs. "At city hall. They were registered with the city planner. Like, your dad, you know?"

I giggle. "And he just gave them to you?"

"Matter of public record, my friend."

"You're brilliant, Celia. Frickin' brilliant."

Celia dials up Becca to invite her over while I buzz Taylor. Her phone goes straight to voice mail, so she's either talking to Ryan and ignoring my interruption or the battery has gone dead. We really need the full team here to go over the deets of Saturday night, so I call Jason, hoping he's finished with basketball practice.

On the fourth ring—so not like Jason to let the phone go that long—he picks up, winded and seemingly exasperated. "I can't talk right now, K. Not a good time."

"That's okay, Jase. I was looking for Taylor. Do you know where she is?"

"She's with me," he says shortly.

Then there's a long pause. One of those pregnant pauses, the kind that crackles across a telephone line and can mean only that the person on the other end has bad news. My hand tingles where it's contacting the cell phone. Energy rushes through me like a lightning bolt, sizzling my nerve endings and activating my psychic vision in a sparkle of blue luminosity.

I see a female lying in a hospital bed, hooked to several life-support machines. An EKG sings out a confirmation of a very weak heartbeat. This person attempted to kill herself. Unsuccessfully, thank the Lord. I see her face ... it's ...

No ... not Taylor. Thank you, Jesus!

"Jason? Oh my God ..."

"You know, don't you, K."

"I think so."

He sniffs hard, fighting back tears, I fear. "My mom's in the ICU, and they say she may not make it through the night."

Mother of God! I nearly drop the phone.

Celia's eyes connect with mine and she knows something's up. She grabs her purse and heads for the door before I can even finish the convo.

"We'll be right there!"

Chapter Six

How can I be such a whiny, selfish little me-me-me'er—"Oh, wah, I've had a bad dream that might come true"—when nothing's even happened to me! Get *over* yourself, Kendall. I mean, Jason and Taylor's mom is clinging to life at Radisson Memorial Hospital after an attempted drug overdose.

Like, she could die!

Like, Jason and Taylor could be orphans. (Well, not technically, since their dad is alive and well and living in Alaska.)

But seriously!

A drug overdose? That's something you only read about online. Or see on an episode of *Maury*. It's a throwaway news item about something that happens to other people in other towns . . . far away. Not an event that occurs in the lives of one of your best friends and your boyfriend.

"Is Mrs. Tillson going to be okay?" Celia whispers to me.

Even though I'm not a doctor, I know she's going to pull through; she got here to the hospital in the nick of time. I see Taylor in my mind, discovering her mother's limp body in the living room. Poor Taylor! What a horrid thing to experience.

"I'm waiting for Jason to finish talking to the doctor," I say to Celia.

Up ahead in the corridor, through the sliding glass doors that separate the ICU from the waiting room, I see that Taylor is clinging to her taller twin brother as the doctor relays information to them. Taylor, the bubbliest person I know, the girl who lets nothing get in her way or keep her down, is inconsolable. I can see that she's racked with sobs, and Jason is doing his best to comfort her.

After a moment, the doctor pats Jason on the shoulder and rubs Taylor's hair affectionately. My senses tell me that this is their family doctor, the man who's been taking care of the twins since they were little. He's almost as devastated by this turn of events as the Tillson kids. The doctor walks off, and Jason releases Taylor so he can sit on a nearby couch. I watch as he puts his head in his hands and begins to cry. Taylor sits next to him, wraps her arms around his shoulders, and rests her blond head on his slumped back.

"Holy shit," Celia says. "Did their mom die?"

"No," I say emphatically. "But it's not good."

I want to go to them both, let them know we're here for them. They aren't even aware of our presence yet. We'll give them a little more time together.

A wave of guilt crashes around me like a mighty tsunami hitting the beach. Suddenly, I feel like this is my fault. Not like I gave her the pills or what have you, but if I hadn't been so focused on myself, maybe I would have seen this coming. I could have warned my friends that their mom was shaky and troubled. Something . . . anything to help.

Don't do that to yourself, Kendall.

I need Emily to piss off right now.

Becca rushes around the corner, nearly out of breath. "I got here as soon as I could. There's, like, no parking at this hospital." She glances about in search of the Tillsons. "Any news?"

"We're waiting," Celia says, squeezing my hand. I wasn't even aware we'd clasped fingers on our arrival at the hospital.

A nurse hustles by with a stack of charts, headed into the ICU.

"Excuse me, ma'am," I call out. "Is there any way we can see our friends, who are just through those doors?"

The nurse turns toward the Tillsons and then back to me. "Aren't you Sarah Moorehead's daughter?"

"Yes, ma'am. How did you know?" Is there yet another psychic in town?

"Kendall, right. I'm Erma Jean Wamback. I work part-time in Dr. Murphy's office with your mama, and I've seen your picture on her desk."

"Oh, right. She's mentioned your name."

"Y'all are friends of Rachel Tillson?" Erma Jean asks.

Celia answers. "Her kids are our best friends. Is there any way we can see them?"

Erma Jean nods her head at the sliding glass door. "If y'all just be quiet, it should be okay."

God bless small-town living.

Without wasting another second, the three of us forge ahead to Jason and Taylor, trying our best not to make a ruckus.

"Oh, you guys," I nearly wail, unable to control my emotions. Jason lifts his head and turns his blue eyes to me. We come together in seconds and embrace. He's never hugged me to him this tightly, as if grasping me will make all the hurt go away. I kiss him next to his ear and whisper softly, "I'm here for you, sweetie."

A wet tear from Jason touches my cheek as we're pressed together. I just rock him back and forth as the emotions of the day drain from him. Over my shoulder, I see Taylor being embraced by both Celia and Becca and crying as hard as her brother. I smile at her, not knowing what else to do.

"I-I-I can't believe she-she-she tried to kill herself," Taylor manages to get out between sobs. "I found her when I got home from yearbook and she-she-she wasn't moving. I called nine one one and just prayed as hard as I could until they got there."

"What did they do to her?" Becca asks, always needing the gory details of everything.

Taylor sips in some air. "They said she wasn't breathing and made me leave the room. I called Jason and tried not to freak out." Her tears begin flowing harder. "I guess I'm freaking out now."

Jason pushes back from me, but not away, lacing his fingers through mine. He reaches out for his sister with his other hand, bringing her close inside his protective hug. "We don't know what happened, Tay. She may have only accidentally taken too many of her pills."

Erma Jean joins all of us and passes over a box of tissues to Taylor. "Why don't y'all go down to the cafeteria and get some Cokes or something? I just checked on your mama and she's in stable condition but still unconscious. It's going to be a while before she wakes up."

"Can't we stay with her?" Taylor asks.

"Sure thing, honey," Erma Jean says. "But why don't you get some air and collect yourself first. Is there a family member who can come get y'all?"

Taylor shakes her mane of hair to indicate no.

"I called Dad," Jason admits.

"You what?"

"Yeah, Tay. I had no choice. What was I supposed to do?"

"What's *he* supposed to do?" she asks. "He left her months ago."

"He's still her husband," Jason says. "And our father. Do you want them to, like, put us in a foster home or separate us or something?"

Taylor drops her eyes. "I hadn't thought of that."

Erma Jean pipes up. "Kendall, I called your mama. She's headed over here soon and said she'll do everything she can to help."

"That's really sweet," Taylor says through a fresh sheen of tears.

"Come on," Celia suggests, "let's go to the cafeteria and wait for Kendall's mom. Milk shakes on me, to calm the nerves."

A weak smile crosses Taylor's lips and she wraps her arm around Celia. Becca follows, and Jason and I bring up the rear going down the long white hallway. Fifteen minutes later, we're seated at a table finishing our cold drinks when Mom rushes in to find us. Behind her is Jason's best friend, Jim Roach; Jim's dad; and Taylor's boyfriend, Ryan MacKenzie. Taylor launches herself into Ryan's arms and starts to cry again.

"You poor things," Mom starts. "I'm so sorry about this."

"Thanks, Mrs. Moorehead," Jason says, polite to a fault. He fills her in on what he knows about his mom's condition.

Mom smoothes his hair across his forehead, such a parental move. I can tell she cares about him, though, because he means so much to me. "I talked to Dr. Strasberg and he says your mom is in stable condition, but they're watching her very closely. You have to do that when it's suspected that someone tried to take her own life."

I can see how difficult it was for Mom to actually say that. She's a professional though. She's birthed babies and informed loved ones of untimely passings. As an emergency room nurse in Chicago, she saw it all and did everything—as much as any doctor had to do.

"Your mom took too much of the medication that she's using for her depression. The doctors want to keep her for several days, as you can imagine."

"When can we see her?" Taylor asks.

"We'll go up right now," Mom says. "Someone said your father has been called?"

"Yes, ma'am," Jason says with a nod. "I talked to him about an hour ago. Thing is, he doesn't know how soon he can get here. He's, like, at this remote location of the park where they dropped him off by seaplane. He has to wait until they can come back and get him. It's totally screwed up. I mean, I had to talk to him through this radio because his cell phone doesn't work. Thing is, he said he'd do his best to get here as soon as he can."

Taylor crosses her arms over her chest and harrumphs. "Typical."

Jason lowers his head. "Come on, Tay . . ."

Mr. Roach steps forward. "If there's anything Norma and I can do for the kids . . ."

"They'll need a place for the night," Mom tells him. "Taylor, you're welcome to stay with us. Maybe you guys can let Jason stay with you?"

"Absolutely," Jim says.

Jason gives him a halfhearted fist bump. "Thanks, man."

Jim nods. "I got your back, dude."

Mom hugs Taylor to her. "Let's go see your mom and then we'll swing by your house and pick up enough clothes for school and the next few days. Whatever you need."

I watch as my friends walk along with my mother, listening intently to her calming voice. Taylor glances back and me and smiles her thanks. She's so fragile right now, someone who's usually so self-confident and sure of herself. I catch up with her and hug her to me.

"I'm scared of what's going to happen to us," she whispers.

"We're going to take care of you, that's what."

"No, I mean . . . after." She takes a deep breath. "Nothing's ever going to be the same. Ever."

I try to latch on to her thoughts or to see what's ahead for her future. It's quite hazy. Always is when it comes to anything that has to do with Jason. We're connected, but I can't get any kind of psychic readings on him. It apparently goes for Taylor too.

"I know, hon . . . I know." I try to reassure her. What do I know, though? I'm just a kid like her.

"Maybe Daddy'll come back to Radisson."

"At least for the time being," I say. "You've got a place with me, though, for as long as you need it."

"Thanks, Kendall. You're such a good friend to me."

"Anything for you, Tay."

So, due to the circumstances, we've opted to postpone our ghost-hunting efforts at Mayor Shy's house until next weekend. Celia thought we should go ahead with it to help Taylor keep her mind off things, but my mom frowned on doing an investigation while a team member's mother was lying in the ICU. She has a point.

I'm sitting in study hall with Becca, racing her at online sudoku, while Celia continues her Internet search of all things

Emily Faulkner related. I can't even think about Emily right now. Taylor cried herself to sleep last night lying next to me in bed. Emily may have been there, for all I know; however, I was too concerned about my friend to pay attention to some obstinate ghost with secrets she doesn't care to share with someone she claims to love. What*ever*. Taylor thrashed around most of the night, so neither of us got much sleep.

The lack of slumber shows in her pretty face—the hollow eyes, dark circles, and downturned mouth. Of course, if my mom had tried to end her life and I'd found her on the living room carpet, I might be a bit sullen myself.

As I'm about to finish an expert-level sudoku puzzle, my phone buzzes out a text message. It's Jason.

> U c Tay?

> I'm in study hall.

> Can't find her anywhere.

> So?

> Worried @ her!

> She's ok

> U don't no that!

It's obvious that Jason's overprotective gene has kicked into double overdrive. I can't blame him, though.

When the bell rings, Jason's at my locker, concern painted across his handsome face. "I still can't find her," he proclaims.

"Calm down. She's at school. What can happen to her?"

He begins to pace. "You don't understand, Kendall."

"Sure I do. I'm the one who listened to her cry all night."

He stops and turns. "Why didn't you tell me that? Why didn't she tell me that? I haven't seen her all day."

I try to reassure him. "She's here. We came to school together in my car."

Not knowing any better, Celia jumps into the convo. "I didn't see Taylor in chemistry class. Maybe she ditched to have some time to herself."

Behind Jason's back, I mouth at Celia, *Not helping!*

Jason whips out his phone and dials his sister's number. "Straight to voice mail."

"Jason, it's going to be . . ." I trail off. Is it really going to be okay?

He glares at me like it's my fault that he can't find his sister. "I'm going to the office to see if she's counted as absent today."

I grab at his shirtsleeve. "Don't do that. What if she is cutting? You want to get her in trouble?"

"Damn right I do!"

Good Lord.

Fortunately, the bell for last period sounds out and we all scatter to our respective classrooms, like cockroaches taking cover in a suddenly lit-up room. Gross analogy, I know, but it works here. Jason storms off toward the gym with cell phone in hand. He's *not* a happy boy right now. My intuition tells me that Taylor's okay . . . she just needs some space. It's not every day that a teenager has to deal with what she's juggling. I'm not going to tell her what to do.

When school's over for the day, I gather my weekend

homework and head out to the parking lot, where I see Taylor leaning against the Fit.

"Where you been, *chica?*" I ask, trying not to sound like a concerned parent.

She raises her shoulders and then lets them slump back into place. Her Nikon D40 camera hangs from her neck, and her right hand rests on top of the lens cannon as if it's a life preserver for her. "I needed some space."

"I understand."

"It was such a pretty day, I just sort of ended up walking around and taking pictures of Radisson. There's so much to see when you look through the camera. So many angles and views you never imagined. I even went to the cemetery and took some shots that I'm going to convert to black-and-white. They turned out *très magnifique* and will make a great addition on the Ghost Huntress website and my portfolio."

We rest against the side of my car and scroll through the many digital images that Taylor took today. She really is an amazing photographer and I know she'll be able to do something with it in her future. The way she frames the shot, it's almost like she's got a psychic eye and can see the result before she snaps the button.

I'm about to comment on a wicked angle of a grave marker with sun flares when Jason comes storming across the parking lot bellowing at the top of his lungs.

"Where the *hell* have you been, Taylor? I've been looking for you everywhere!" She staves him off with her hands, but he's not having any of it. "It's not bad enough that Mom's lay-ing in the ICU fighting for her life—you have to pull a disap-pearing act like you're some sort of toddler who's run away from home."

She arches up defensively like I've never seen before. "How dare you talk to me like that?"

"I'm your older brother and I'll say what I want. You had me scared shitless."

Taylor flattens her lips. "Well, get over yourself. You're not in charge of me."

He reaches for her upper arm. "I am when Mom is inca-pacitated and Dad is halfway across the continent."

Stupidly, I comment, "Your dad will be here soon, right?"

Jason's blue eyes darken to a near navy color as he tells me nonverbally to butt out.

"You're not my keeper, Jason Tillson," Taylor shouts. Tears begin to escape her eyes. "And you're not the only one hurt and upset over Mom. Was it *you* who found her? No! Was it *you* who had to call nine one one? No! Was it *you* who rode in the ambulance with her? No! It was me . . . all three of those things. So, I think you need to just . . . just . . . *ne me dites pas quoi faire!*"

Jason is stunned, as am I. I don't have to be psychic—or French—to know that Taylor just told him to back off and leave her alone, and how!

"Taylor!"

It's too late. She spins on her heels and runs off toward the gym, no doubt looking for Ryan.

I feel I need to help. "The more you push her, the more defiant she'll become. Just let her handle this in her own way, Jason."

"What do you know, Kendall?" Jason doesn't mean to snap at me, I'm sure, although I'm the target of his pent-up frustrations. "You have two parents that are still together. You have a mom that's okay. One that hasn't been seeking plastic surgery to change herself and psychotherapy to deal with the desertion of her husband."

"I know that, Jase—"

"Don't tell me how to deal with my sister and we'll be fine." He follows in Taylor's wake and I choose *not* to follow.

At home, later, Taylor decides to join us for dinner. Dad's working late and Kaitlin's spending the night at Penny Carmickle's, so it's just us girls and Mom. It's a quiet dinner with questions of how the day was, how Taylor's mom is doing (still unconscious), and what our plans are for tonight.

"We have a bunch of movies from Netflix," Mom says. "Why don't you girls stay in tonight? You can pop some popcorn and turn the lights off."

"That sounds like fun. What do you think, Taylor?"

She pushes her butter beans around on her plate—which I don't blame her for—and gives a half smile. "Sure. Whatever."

This is not the Taylor I know. Then again, her life was drastically altered yesterday.

We help Mom clean the dirty dinner dishes and then retire to my room with a bowl of freshly popped Orville, gigamonic Diet Cokes, and the red envelopes full of movies. I slip in *Moulin Rouge*—a favorite I can never get enough of—and settle into the pillows propped at the foot of my bed.

Taylor, however, changes into a fresh pair of jeans from her suitcase and pulls a brush through her long hair.

"What are you doing?" I ask.

"I have to get out," she says in a huffed breath.

I sit up. "Is it something I did? Something I said?"

"No, Kendall! You're amazing. It's not you. Anything but. I just . . . I need to—"

Just then, a small rock pings on my window. WTF? I bound out of bed to see what the deal is. When I look down, there stands Ryan MacKenzie in his letter jacket, waving for me to open up.

"Is Taylor ready?" he asks in a loud whisper.

"Are you kidding me?"

She brushes past me. "Don't hate me, Kendall." She gives me a European goodbye, one kiss on each cheek like we've just met at a café in Paris for a latte. "Whatever you do, don't tell Jase, okay?"

"Ummm . . ."

"Promise!" Then she climbs out the window onto the awning and shimmies over to the post that holds the front porch. Has she been practicing to be on *Survivor* or something with moves like that?

"How will you get back in?" I call down as quietly as I can.

"Leave the door unlocked. I'll be in before dawn."

And then she and Ryan are off into the darkness. Son of a bitch. What the hell am I supposed to do? Make a fake Taylor to stuff into my bed in case Mom comes in to check on us? My friend has made me an accomplice, whether she realizes it or not.

I say a quick prayer requesting protection for Taylor, that Mom doesn't come a-knocking, and forgiveness if I have to lie to her or Jason. Mostly, I pray that we can all just get through this. That Mrs. Tillson comes out of her coma. That Mr. Tillson can bring his family back together when he finally gets picked up from the frickin' wilderness tundra of Alaska.

And most of all, I pray that I can avoid the Tillson drama and not be drawn into the middle.

That's a lose-lose situation.

CHAPTER SEVEN

THANKFULLY, TAYLOR IS SOUND ASLEEP next to me when I rise Saturday morning. I don't want to know where she's been or what time she slipped through the back door to return to my bedroom undetected. No questions asked when she wakes up, yawns, and stretches next to me and my cats Eleanor and Buckley. The kitties could care less that there's an extra person in bed with us as long as they still have room to spread out.

Taylor scratches Eleanor behind her tabby ear and asks, "Did you tell Jase anything?"

I shake my head into my pillow. "We talked briefly last night and texted a little. I told him we were watching movies and having a girls' night. That seemed to appease him."

Taylor closes her eyes and sighs. "Thanks, Kendall."

"What are friends for?"

We dress, grab a quick snack that Mom left for us, and then head over to Radisson Memorial Hospital.

"Any change?" Taylor asks when we approach the nurses' station.

A tall, slender black woman turns and smiles at us. Her

nametag reads *Lucinda*. "You must be the Tillson girl. Your mama was asking for you a little while ago."

"She's awake?" Taylor exclaims and grabs for my hand. Tears immediately squeeze from the corners of her eyes as her grin spreads across her face. "Oh my God, Kendall! She's awake!"

I grip her hand tightly in support of the good news.

"Well, she was awake earlier," Lucinda explains. "She's gone back to sleep, though."

Taylor slumps next to me, all of the joy momentarily spent. "Oh."

"No, sweetie," the nurse says. "Don't fret. Her vitals are looking good and her heartbeat is strong. The doctor checked on her a little while ago and was pleased with her progress."

"Thank God," I say. "Can we see her?"

Lucinda nods and points us toward Mrs. Tillson's room.

We enter the darkened room as silently as we can and Taylor takes a seat in the middle of her bed. She reaches for her hand and weaves her fingers through the still ones of her mother.

"Oh, Mama." Taylor speaks in a whisper. "Why did you do it?" When her mother doesn't move or respond, my friend lifts her eyes to me. "Can you tell me? Do *you* know?"

I reach over and take Mrs. Tillson's hand and concentrate. I breathe through the sliver of knowledge being shown to me. Rachel Tillson got a phone call from her Delta Air Lines pilot boyfriend. He wanted to make a clean break with her because he had decided to reconcile with his wife for the sake of their four kids. Mrs. Tillson felt used and unattractive, seeing as how she'd lost *two* men, and she didn't think she had anything to live for anymore.

As the vision clears, my resentment amplifies. Didn't have anything to live for? Are you kidding me? How about two "things" named Jason and Taylor? I bite down my anger toward their mother, trying only to be a reassurance to my friends. But come on! Damn . . . sometimes being psychic and knowing things that others don't know is a real frickin' burden, 'cause you can't just blurt out the truth. That saying about sticks and stones may break your bones but words will never hurt you is total bullshit. Words are forever . . . and they sting. I will not hurt my friend or kick her when she's down.

Instead of sharing the info, I look at Taylor and say, "It's not really clear to me. I'm sure your mom will tell you everything when she's doing better. The important thing is to be here for her. Let her know you're around and that you love her."

"I do love her. So much," Taylor says.

There's movement at the door. It's Jason. His hair is mussed and he doesn't look like he's slept much. His RHS sweatshirt is inside out, and his face seems long and sad. He steps into the room, joins Taylor at their mother's bed, and takes his sister's free hand.

His beautiful blue eyes lock on mine. I smile, trying to let my love for him shine out. He winks back.

"Talk to her, Jason," I say softly.

"She's asleep," he says.

"She'll wake up again. She needs to know that *both* of you are here."

He turns back to his mother. "I love you, Mom. Don't leave us. Whatever's wrong, we can work through it. We always do."

Rachel Tillson's eyelids flutter open and her soft blue eyes focus on her two children in the room with her. I watch as she swallows hard and weakly licks her lips. "J-J-Jason. Tay-baby."

"Mommy," Taylor says in a childish squeak.

Jason moves to the head of his mom's bed and runs his fingers through her hair.

With that, I quietly sneak out of the room, leaving the siblings with their mom. Whatever happens, they'll make it . . . together.

"Is it okay to admit that I'm happy *not* to be investigating the mayor's house tonight, crawling around God knows where trying to capture EVPs or get infrared pictures?" Celia says to me over the roar of the crowd.

"I'll second that," Becca says and then crams a handful of popcorn into her mouth.

"It's good to be out of Radisson for a little bit," Taylor chimes in.

The four of us drove in my car from Radisson to Felcher's Point, where RHS is taking on the Felcher Falcons in roundball—a term Jason and his buddies use for basketball. He and Ryan are both on the team, so we're riveted to the action.

I have to agree with Celia, quite frankly. It's been a hell of a week and I'm mentally exhausted. My heart's not into ghost hunting at the moment, although I do still want to find out what's going on inside the mayor's mansion. Right now, some mindless spectator sporting is what does the body good. Plus, any opportunity to gawk at Jason Tillson in his basketball uniform is time well spent.

"Good shot, Ryan!" Taylor shouts, backing it up with a hearty clap.

The cheerleaders, led by my former nemesis turned polite acquaintance Courtney Langdon, move from the front row of the bleachers out to the middle of the court to do a pyramid during the time-out. I glance over at Jason kneeling on one knee and swabbing his drenched face with a white towel. The weight of the world is on his young shoulders, yet he's playing like a champion. He's already got twelve points, and RHS is up by three.

When the action resumes, Ryan MacKenzie is fouled by the Falcons with only a few seconds left in the game. Stephanie Crawford, a friend of mine on the squad, begins to cheer, and we all join in.

"Up in the air, round the rim, come on, Ryan, put it in! Sink it! Sink it! Come on, Ryan, sink it!"

He nails the first shot, nearly stripping the net. All of us RHS faithful who traveled to the game are on our feet. When Ryan misses the second shot and it bounces off the rim, Jason snags the rebound and slams the ball home. Why am I not surprised? Not because I know what an awesome player he is—which he is—but because a minute before it happened, I had a bit of a déjà vu moment where I saw Jason move in for the slam-dunk kill. It's the first time I've ever really had a connection to something Jason based, and my soul tingles in delight knowing we've bonded on such a cosmic level. Of course, Jason would merely roll his eyes at me if I told him. So, instead, I join the rest of the RHSers in flooding the Falcons' floor to congratulate our team.

When Jason sees me, he picks me up in his strong grip and holds me close to his sweaty body. He's got that boy ick smell to him, but I don't care. There's more to this embrace than the simple victory of a high school basketball team. Jason's thanking me for this morning as well. Words don't have to be exchanged . . . I just know.

"We're all headed back to Radisson after we change," he tells me. "After the team bus drops us off, I'll get my Jeep. Then meet up with us at Finnian's Restaurant, okay?" He leans in for a quick kiss that tastes salty.

"Sure thing," I manage to say in my swoony state. I find my posse and ask if they're ready to go.

"I'm gonna ride with Dragon," Becca says. Dragon's actually Brent Dragisich, her boyfriend, who decided to show up at the game even though he'd told her earlier that it was "lame."

"You sure?"

"Yeah, no prob. Where are y'all meeting up?" she asks.

"Finnian's."

"See ya there."

I turn to Celia. "Where's Taylor?"

Celia points to an older couple. "She's with Ryan's parents, over there. He's not taking the bus back to Radisson, so she's gonna ride with them."

I crinkle my smile. "Looks like it's just you and me, kid."

Celia laughs and we head back out to my car.

Fifteen minutes later, we're returning to Radisson on the winding back roads. "Why didn't we follow the team bus and take the interstate?"

Celia looks at her cell phone. "The GPS said this way was quicker."

I roll my eyes at her and keep driving. Such a techno geek. If it lights up, beeps, or connects to the Internet, Celia Nichols *must* have it in her possession. And I'm not convinced that the GPS is all that it's cracked up to be. Why in the world would it take us on County Road 215 when just twenty miles down the road there's a perfectly good interstate highway that President Eisenhower took a lot of trouble to have built for us.

Whatev. "Crank up that Kaskade CD. I just got the new one and it's totally awesome."

Celia inserts the disk into my player and we jam out as I concentrate on the dimly lit road with the thick yellow lines.

"So, did I tell you about this new piece of equipment I've ordered?" Celia asks. "It's called the Ovilus and we can use it in our investigations."

"A what?"

"Ovilus. It's made by this guy who's a former engineer. It's got an array of sensors that detect various environmental conditions. It adds all of the data together and equates that value with a word from the dictionary."

"Whoa, Geek Girl. That's way over my head," I say with a laugh. "In English, please?"

Celia snickers. "It has a dictionary that will speak out, and supposedly it's spirits coming through. I had Loreen order one because the guy doesn't like to sell to underage people. She's going to learn how to use it and bring it on our next investigation."

"Okay, that sounds cool. Just another tool in our ghost-hunting kit. Just like me," I say. Celia's always referring to me as a tool in her ghost-hunting kit.

"Absomalutely," she says. "He's got a website called Digital-Dowsing.com—he's looking to make you and your pendulum obsolete."

"Never," I say firmly.

"You should check out his website. He's got this other thing called the paranormal puck that—oh my God, Kendall! Watch out!"

Celia's bloodcurdling scream scares the holy shit out of me and I blink hard to focus on the road ahead. Out of nowhere, a deer has suddenly appeared in the middle of the winding road, its eyes shining with the reflection of my headlights. I jerk the wheel to the left and concentrate on keeping the Fit on the road and not in the nearby ditch as I try to avoid slamming into Bambi's mom and making her a permanent fixture on my hood.

Celia's got the sissy bar firmly in her grip, and both of our seat belts lock up, pulling us snugly back into the bucket seats. I apply the brakes firmly, just like my driver's ed teacher taught me, and try not to panic as I bring the car to a stop. The road is deserted save for us and the near-roadkill. The deer eyeballs me with something resembling street attitude in her face and then scampers across the road to safety.

My breathing is staggered and I find it hard to steady it. Tears sting at the back of my eyes, but I won't let them fall. I did everything I was supposed to do. I kept the car under control and no one was hurt. I've seen pictures of what deer can do to automobiles. We just dodged a huge venison-filled bullet.

"Jesus, Kendall. That was close. Good driving," Celia exclaims. She peels her hand off the sissy bar and takes a deep breath.

Before I can get my own breathing back to normal, I'm struck blind by a vision. White light flashes in my face like a thousand headlights. Screeches and screams fill my ears. "Jason! No!"

"Kendall, what's wrong?" Celia shouts, trying to snap me back.

I throw her arm off me. "I see it, clear as day. Oh God! Not Jason."

Celia nearly begs. "Stop, Kendall! It's okay."

It's *not* okay! "Jason's at the wheel of his Jeep. Something's wrong. Something's happened to him. I can't see it clearly, but I know I have to get to him."

"Whoa, girlfriend." Celia reaches out to me again. "It's just a vision, Kendall. It'll be okay. Shake it off. We had a close call with the deer and nothing else. We both had on our seat belts and you're a damn good driver, so all is well."

I blink hard, regaining my sight after the vision. Emily materializes in the back seat with a look on her face that I can only describe as *relieved*. I feel almost like her hands had been on the wheel with mine, helping me steer away from trouble.

I thank her silently in my mind. She smiles and fades away.

"All right. Let's get going," I say, feeling as composed as I'm going to be.

"The GPS says we're twelve miles from Radisson."

"Oh, the hell with your GPS," I say. "I'm following the road signs."

We enter the city limits fifteen minutes later and pull into the parking lot of Finnian's Restaurant. Instead of a celebratory gathering of RHSers, there seems to be some sort of ruckus, and Jason Tillson's Jeep is the center of everything.

Holy shit . . . did my vision come true?

I slam the parking brake on and jump out of the car, barely getting the key out of the ignition. Jason's standing outside of the Jeep, doubled over, huffing and puffing and gasping for breath.

"Jason!"

"Kendall! Thank God you're okay!"

Kyle Kadish calls out, "Dude, good thing *you're* okay. That could have been gnarly!"

I rush to Jason's side and we hug like nobody's business. "I saw something bad happening to you," I say quickly. "Tell me nothing's wrong."

Jason looks me squarely in the eye, shock covering his handsome face. "No effing way. I almost got plowed by an eighteen-wheeler just now turning into the parking lot. The guy totally ran the red light and almost slammed the Jeep."

I'm on the verge of tears. This is too much for a seventeen-year-old to take. "I'm so glad you're okay."

"It wasn't all the trucker's fault," Sean Carmickle chimes in. "Tillson, I was riding with you. Your mind was three counties away. What the hell?"

On my tiptoes, I glance up at my boyfriend. "Jason?"

"I couldn't help it, K. I was distracted because something told me that you were in danger. I don't know who it was or where it came from. It was enough to jar my attention away from driving and I almost didn't see that damn truck."

"Good thing Kadish screamed like a twelve-year-old girl," Sean says with a snicker.

Kyle reaches over and pops Sean on the shoulder, kiddingly, but I see nothing funny about any of this.

"Celia and I almost hit a deer," I admit. "Like, it could have been bad."

"Kendall . . ." Jason's face reads pure fright. I'm sure mine mirrors his. "What does this mean?"

I'm not a hundred percent sure, but I suspect that there's a cosmic connection between Jason and me that's deeper than either of us realize.

I don't have a clue what to do about it, so I just close my eyes and hold on tightly to him for as long as I can.

Celia doesn't miss a heart beat. "That's some deep shit."

"You said a mouthful, my friend."

CHAPTER EIGHT

THE MASS ENDS A LITTLE EARLY SUNDAY MORNING, so I hang behind in the church while Father Massimo talks to the exiting parishioners. His sermon was about total faith in God and not living in fear of the unknown. Geesh—was he preaching directly to me?

"Hey, Kendall. How's everything going with the ghost hunting?" Father Massimo asks as he reenters the sanctuary. He's tall with jet-black hair and dark eyes to match. I can see why Loreen might be falling for him—he's cute, in an older guy sort of way. I mean, he's like in his midthirties!

"Hey there, Father." Trying to keep it light, I ask, "How was your hot date with Loreen?"

Did my Episcopal priest just blush? Too cute!

"She's a nice lady and I enjoy spending time with her," he says with a slight smirk. I can see he's not going to satiate my need for gossip.

"Is that what you old people are calling it these days? Spending time?" I giggle and twist away from his playful swat.

His mood darkens and he frowns black brows at me. "I

know you didn't stay after church to ask me about my love life. I know you, Kendall Moorehead. Something's bothering you. Do you need more holy water for your investigations?"

"No, sir," I say, switching gears. "I do need advice, though."

"That's what I'm here for," he says with a smile.

We move up to the choir loft and sit together on the hard benches where I pour my heart out to him, telling him everything, from the dream/vision of Emily, then the one of my death, and finally to what happened last night, when Jason and I both avoided accidents at the exact same time.

"What's going on, Father? I'm literally afraid of my own shadow now."

"Kendall, with your finding you psychic abilities and subsequent ghost hunting, you've really opened yourself up to the angels, the universe . . . to anyone that wants to reach out and contact you. You're a magnet to those who have messages to get through. I do believe God gave you these abilities so you can help others, not for you to fear what might happen to you." He reaches over and takes my hand. "You're a strong girl, Kendall. Loreen and I have both seen it. You've embraced your talents and you've cultivated more along the way. Look at all of the lost souls you and your group have helped so far. You can't let fear of the unknown get you down."

My hand shakes underneath his and I try to calm my nerves. That close call with the deer last night really freaked me out. It seems that I need to spend all my energies and efforts on being safe. I'm obsessed with it.

Father Mass obviously picks up on this. "Kendall, you need to let go and let God."

I snicker. "That's not from the Bible, that's from Alcoholics Anonymous, isn't it?"

He cocks his head to the side. "It's the message that counts. Come on, where's the spunky gal I know who doesn't let anything get her down?"

I bite my lip, then say, "She's had hell and four dollars scared out of her."

My priest stands and points his finger at me. "Then I think you need to stop obsessing and find other interests in your life besides ghost hunting. While being psychic will always be a part of who you are, it's doesn't have to be everything, Kendall. Join a club at school. Find a new hobby. Something to take your mind off death. Anything done to extreme is detrimental to one's state of mind. Try it tomorrow, Kendall. Trust me. It'll help."

How can I not trust him? He's a priest.

"Okay, I'll try."

"I don't know how I let you talk me into this," I mutter to Taylor Monday after school. I mentioned to her last night the thing that Father Mass said about finding other interests, and damn if Taylor didn't drag me into her after-school world.

Yearbook.

I don't exactly know what I can offer the RHS annual. I've got zero talent in photography, my writing is only good enough for English papers and other school assignments, and I wouldn't know a good page layout if it bit me on the nose. I certainly don't have the social connections here at school to help out with the gossip fodder, so I can't see this being very productive for me.

"You must be Kendall," a cute brunette with dark brown glasses says to me. She's holding a clipboard with an authoritative grip, and I know she must be some big muckety-muck on the yearbook staff.

Extending my right hand, I shake her outstretched one in a very professional manner. "Kendall Moorehead at your service."

"Great to have you here, Kendall. Taylor's told me all about you. I'm Shelby-Nichole Holt, yearbook editor." She flips her dark brown hair over her shoulder and smiles at me. "Fresh blood is always welcome around here, and I think I've got *just* the committee for you."

A cocktail of trepidation and excitement shakes me as I await Shelby-Nichole's verdict for my assignment.

"Over here, Kendall." Shelby-Nichole points to a table occupied by a guy with a neon green skateboard across the front of his black T-shirt; his blond hair just touches the top of his eyebrows. "This is Colton Powell," she says. "He's our number-one ad salesman. He'll show you the ropes."

I cringe inwardly. "Ads?"

"Yeah, the annual is paid for by sponsors, parents, and local businesses that purchase advertising space in the back." Shelby-Nichole picks up a copy of last year's RHS *Rambler* yearbook. She flips to the end where there are tens of pages of print ads from various sources.

Crap! I've never been good at selling anything. When I was back in Chicago, our church choir sold poinsettias around Christmastime to raise money for a trip. I sold exactly two: one to my mother and one to my Grandma Ethel. Not quite salesman-of-the-year material.

I think of what Father Mass told me, though, that I need to try my hand at something new. So I let out the breath I've been holding and look at Shelby-Nichole. "Whatever you think is best," I say with a forced smile.

"Great! Colton, this is Kendall. Show her the ropes!"

He stands and I see he's a bit shorter than I am. His jeans are baggy, and he has worn sneakers with scuff marks all over them. He must notice that I'm checking him out, so he says, "I'm a skateboarder," to explain his casual appearance.

"Oh, that's cool," I say.

Shelby-Nichole puts Colton in a headlocking hug. "Colton here sold almost eighty percent of our ads last year. Of course, it helped that I got my dad to have the city buy a two-page spread."

Colton rolls his eyes and shrugs off Shelby-Nichole's compliment. "No big."

"Who's your dad?" I ask the editor.

She adjusts her glasses on the bridge of her nose and seems

melancholy for a moment. "Oh, well, like, my dad died not too long ago. Mayer Holt. He was the mayor of Radisson."

My wide-open mouth registers my surprise. "You're Donn's daughter?"

"Stepdaughter . . . although she's, like, the only mom I've ever known. Donn married my dad when I was five. My mom died of cancer right after I was born," Shelby-Nichole explains.

For a second, I glance around Shelby-Nichole to see if the spirits of her mother and father are still with her. Her aura is clear, though, and I don't sense any guides with her, which means her folks are at peace. If only everyone could find such bliss. Then again, I wouldn't be a ghost huntress. Speaking of . . .

"My team and I are supposed to do an investigation at your house," I say. "Things got weird last weekend with—" I glance across the room at Taylor, who is scrolling through some digital pictures on the computer with a couple of fellow staffers looking on. "Well, Taylor's mom is in the hospital and we had to rearrange our schedule."

Shelby-Nichole nods and lowers her voice. "How's Taylor doing? That can't be easy for her."

I lift my arms and shrug. "As good as can be expected. She's been crashing with me, so I'm trying to help her through it. We're still waiting for her dad to get in from Alaska. He's had some, shall we say, aerodynamic challenges." Jason found out a big snowstorm hit the area where his dad is, so no telling when we'll see him.

"Poor thing. It's hard when your home's all busted up,"

Shelby-Nichole says with an almost adult tsk-tsk in her voice. "Seems that's more the norm than the exception these days."

Colton clears his throat and picks up a fishing magazine. "Y'all let me know when you want to get to work." He smirks at us and then buries himself in a story about tuna fishing near oil rigs in the Gulf of Mexico.

Shelby-Nichole just waves him off and keeps talking. "Donn told me y'all are gonna do an investigation at the house and I can't wait."

"Why's that?"

She searches around to make sure no one else is listening, like she's got this big secret to tell. "I have been hearing weird footsteps coming from the attic since we all moved in, eight years ago. There's nothing up there but a bunch of boxes, some old furniture, and our Christmas and other holiday decorations. *You* tell me who's up there moving around."

I'd like to tell her all about the woman I saw in the top-story window, but until Celia, Taylor, Becca, and I can get in there with our equipment, I'm not making any suppositions about anything. The last thing you want to do is tell someone his or her house is haunted without any proof or evidence.

Shelby-Nichole's mouth drops open. "Ooo . . . just had a fabulous idea! We'll do a special one-page feature on your ghost huntresses in the *Rambler* this year."

"I don't know about—"

"Don't be modest," she interrupts. "It'll be easy to do. Maybe I can tag along on your investigation at my house."

A gnawing in my tummy tells me this isn't the smartest thing to agree to. Shelby-Nichole is a little pushy—in a nice way, though—trying to get the feature in her annual. "Why not? Sounds like fun."

"I don't know about fun," she says. "But it'll be interesting. Never a dull moment in that mansion."

"Seriously? Why do you say that?"

"The place gives me the heebie-jeebies," Shelby-Nichole says firmly. "I just crank my music as loud as I can and concentrate on other things. Between my yearbook responsibilities and my volunteer time at the Radisson Retirement Home, I've got a lot to keep me busy."

"That's really great of you, Shelby-Nichole."

Colton lets out a long sigh. "Yo, these ads aren't gonna sell themselves."

Shelby-Nichole laughs and grabs her clipboard from the table. "True, true. Great to have you on staff, Kendall."

"I'll try not to let you down," I say, half joking.

"Sit, Moorehead," Colton says to me. Then he slides over a list of stores in the Radisson area; each business is either highlighted or checked off. "The ones in yellow have committed to ad space already. The ones with the checks need a follow-up." He waggles a tanned finger in my face. "A lot of people are going to tell you no automatically. Don't ever take their no as a final answer. Let them know we're kids and we volunteer our time and that it's the right thing for them to do for the community."

I laugh heartily. "In other words, guilt them into taking out an ad?"

He nods. "You got it, babe. Whatever works. I didn't bring in eighty percent of the revenue last year by taking no for an answer."

A glimpse into Colton Powell's blue eyes, framed behind black-rimmed glasses, gives me a view of his future. Smart kid in math with good grades and an analytical mind. I definitely see dollah signs in his future. Something in the retail industry . . . those guys that calculate trends. I have no idea what the exact terminology is, but he plugs raw sales data into spreadsheets to generate all kinds of graphics, charts, and other corporate crap that makes the fat men in the glass offices squeal with delight. Wow . . . how did I come up with *that?*

"You're going places, Colton," I say, like we've known each other forever.

"Well, thanks, Kendall Moorehead. Now, you get one of those lists and get out there and hit the streets of Radisson. You're going places too."

"Oh, come on, Loreen. It's only a hundred fifty dollars for a quarter page," I say, nearly begging. "Don't you want to support the children of this community?"

Loreen lifts the corner of her mouth and then tries not to snort-laugh. "I think I already support at least one, or four, if you think about your whole group."

"She's right," Father Mass says. He's stretched out on the velvet couch in Divining Woman, wearing jeans and a U2 sweatshirt and sipping a cup of something from Central Perk.

"Why don't you buy an ad on behalf of the church?" Loreen shoots back.

Father Mass shakes his head. "That's up to the bishop of the district."

"Stupid church rules," I mutter. "Sorry, Father."

"No skin off my nose. I don't make the rules."

"Quiet, Mass," Loreen says. "All right, Kendall, sign me up. But only because it's you."

Feeling the need to Snoopy dance in place, I reach for the order book Colton sent with me. My first sale! Excellent! My pulse is racing like I just hit the Mega Millions jackpot.

Loreen digs through her black hole of a purse and pulls out her checkbook. She turns to her boyfriend. "So this was your idea?"

"What? Your buying an ad?"

"No. Kendall working on the yearbook staff."

He shrugs and sips. "I merely suggested she find other interests. I believe it was Taylor Tillson who talked her into yearbook specifically."

"Helllllllo! I'm right here. Quit talking about me like I'm not sitting in front of you." I wink at Loreen and stretch my hand out to accept the check made out to Radisson High School. Maybe I'll give Colton Powell a run for the top ad salesperson.

"Are we investigating Mayor Shy's house this weekend?" Loreen asks.

"Looks that way," I say. "Did you get that Ovulator thing Celia was talking about?"

Loreen tosses her head back as she cracks up. "Not an Ovulator. An Ovilus. And yes, it should be here tomorrow. We'll try it out at the mayor's house to see what we can get."

"You and your toys," Father Mass says, tongue-in-cheek.

Loreen runs her hand over his short-cropped hair in a display of affection.

Whatever. I so don't want to sit here and watch them flirt.

"I heard that," Loreen says to me. Ooops. Forgot she's psychic too and picks up on nearly *all* of my thoughts.

"I think you two are adorable."

"That's better," Loreen says. She reaches over and hugs me and then jumps back as if she's been electrocuted.

I scream as a rush of static energy passes between us, making me itch from the palms of my hands to the soles of my feet. "What the hell was that all about?"

Loreen throws her hands over her mouth to cover her deep gasp. Her eyes dilate; her pupils are humongous. Father Mass is on his feet and in between the two of us before I can take another breath.

"Loreen, honey?" he prompts.

She tosses her strawberry blond curls around her head like she's shaking off annoying bugs. "Make it stop," she says in a whisper.

Mass grabs her arms and tries to pull her to him.

I press for information. "What are you seeing, Loreen?" And why am I not experiencing it too?

Collecting her breath, Loreen reaches out for me. "It was shown to me. Unclear. Confusing." Her breathing is ragged, but she keeps going. "There's a vengeful woman there."

"Where?" Mass and I both ask at the same time.

"At Mayor Shy's." Loreen sucks in air again. "Vengeful. Hateful. Dangerous. We have to proceed with caution."

She's right, Kendall . . .

"Emily?" I call out.

Loreen looks around, wincing from the pain she's feeling through this connection.

A vengeful spirit, indeed. Watch yourself.

I cram my hands into my hair and rub hard at my scalp. "Neither of you can tell me more than that? Come on!"

Loreen collapses into Father Mass's arms and then they sit together on the couch. Emily is nowhere to be seen, although I can feel her presence hovering around me. Why she continues to talk in riddles and innuendoes I don't understand! All I know is that everything in my life seems to center around what may happen at the mayor's house. No matter what awaits me, I've got to face it head on . . . whatever it is.

CHAPTER NINE

JASON PULLS HIS JEEP into the long, winding driveway of Mayor Shy's mansion on Saturday night and then shoves the gearshift into park. His eyes connect with mine in the moonlight.

"I don't want you doing this investigation," he says with authority.

"I have to figure out what's going on, Jason. It's like everything is a tiny puzzle piece and I've got to fit it all together."

"Why you?" he asks with a bit of desperation.

Placing my hand on his slightly stubbled cheek, I say, "Because it's what I'm supposed to do."

He tugs me toward him and hugs me with gusto. "I can't have anything happen to you, Kendall."

Awww . . . "I'll be okay, especially with the whole team here. And you're here, as well as Loreen and Father Mass."

There's a knock on the driver's-side window, and Jason and I jump apart.

"Gotcha!" Becca sings out and waves on her way up the walk.

Jason grits his teeth. "I swear to God . . ."

"Don't," I say and then kiss him quickly. "It's not good to swear to God, especially before an investigation." I reach for my jean jacket and get my rose quartz pendulum from the pocket. "I'm ready if you are."

"I'm never ready for these investigations," Jason mutters.

"Come on, He-Man!"

"Get it over with, Kendall."

He's talking about protection. Never, ever, ever go into an investigation without protection of some sort, whether it be a lucky charm, a blessed cross, holy water, or a favorite stone. For me, I prefer to place holy water on my pulse points and recite Saint Michael's prayer. Jason closes his eyes too as I go through my ritual.

"Saint Michael the archangel, defend us in battle. Be our protection against the wickedness and the snares of the devil. May God rebuke him, we humbly pray, and do thou, O prince of the heavenly host, by the divine power of God, cast into hell Satan and all the evil spirits who roam throughout the world seeking the ruin of souls. Amen."

"Amen," Jason says. "So why do you say that?"

I quirk my mouth to the side. "Because it invokes the archangel Michael to protect us."

"Kendall, I'm Baptist, not Episcopal."

Smacking him on the shoulder, I roll my eyes. "It all works the same. Come on." Then we head into the house.

"Hey, y'all, everyone's in the living room." It's Shelby-Nichole, welcoming us in as if this is some sort of slumber party instead of a paranormal investigation of the house she lives in. Then again, she said she pretty much ignores everything she sees and hears.

We follow her down a long hallway of freshly shined hardwood floors. Portraits of famous Radissonians hang on the walls on either side of us. They seem to be judging me, like I've done something wrong. I suppress the urge to flip them off.

"There y'all are," Celia says. She's decked out in dark jeans, a sweatshirt, and her ghost-hunting vest with the kazillion pockets so she can carry everything with her at once and have it at a moment's notice. "We've got the base camp set up in the kitchen. Becca's got digital recorders all over the place, and Loreen's got the Ovilus with her for us to try."

"Hi, Kendall," Mayor Shy says as she walks into the room holding cans of sodas. Her long blond mane is pulled back into a straight ponytail, and an Atlanta Braves baseball cap is on her head. "I'm quite excited about tonight. It's been an interesting day here."

"How so?" I ask.

Shelby-Nichole pokes herself into the circle. "Donn's assistant left the house screaming today, saying she'd never work here again."

"That sounds odd."

Celia pulls out a small notebook and pen. "Can you give me more details, Mayor?"

"Yeah, sure. Her name is Susan Cummings and she's about

so tall with dark blond hair and—" The mayor stops when Celia holds up her hand.

"No, ma'am, I meant, can you give me more details on the 'interesting' part of the day and why Ms. Cummings won't work here anymore."

Donn peels off her glasses and attends to a smudge on one lens with the end of her fitted shirt. When she plunks the spectacles back on her nose, she looks Celia square in the face. "It's quite simple. Ms. Cummings said something tried to push her down the front stairs and it scared the life out of her."

"Did you see anything?" I ask.

"No, I was out tending my roses," the mayor says.

"I saw something."

All eyes turn to Shelby-Nichole, who stands a foot away.

"What's that, dear?" Donn asks.

"Susan was at the top of the stairs and it was as if she tripped. I saw her catch herself on the railing and then she bolted down the stairs. I asked her what was up and she said she heard a voice snarling in her ear."

"What did it snarl at her?" Celia asks.

Shelby-Nichole gulps down hard, then says, "Revenge."

Donn laughs. "That's just silly, Shelby-Nichole. I'm sure Susan's departure from the mansion today had more to do with her catching her fiancé in bed with that redheaded waitress who works at Café au Lait than with ghosts." Celia, Taylor, and I gasp in unison. "Now, y'all didn't hear that from me."

"Anything you tell us in the course of the investigation is private," Taylor assures her. "Much like the patient-doctor confidentiality."

"All right, then," Donn says. "When can we get started?"

I take a quick peek at my watch and see that it's nearly midnight. Ahh . . . the witching hour, when things that go bump in the night like to come out and play. Or at least that seems to be the case for us during our investigations.

Becca's running a sound check of her equipment and making sure there are plenty of batteries in the voice recorders while Celia inspects the infrared cameras she has set up throughout the manor. Taylor's got her IR camera around her neck and is adjusting the F-stop readings when I approach her from behind.

"Hey, Tay," I say in a whisper, trying not to startle her.

She spins around with a half smile on her face. I can tell the old Taylor is there wanting to burst out with some sort of sassy French colloquialism. The harsh reality is that the scared Taylor is the one showing her face, pretending that nothing is hurting her and she can go about like nothing's wrong. "Cameras are ready to go," she reports.

I simply pat her on the back and rub, letting her know I'm her friend and here for her.

"Where's Loreen?" I ask Celia.

"She's upstairs in the attic getting a feel for the place. Do you want to go up there?"

The attic . . . where I saw the apparition in the window.

Sooner or later I'll have to find out who or what that is. Why not sooner?

"Donn, may we start the investigation in the attic?"

She steps forward. "Be my guest, Kendall."

We all follow the mayor up the winding front staircase, through the second story, and back to the rear of the house, where she opens a small door. Behind it is a tiny wooden staircase leading up to the attic area. I can hear Loreen moving around up there already.

Clump-clump, clump-clump, clump-clump.

It's like the sound of a ballet slipper scraping against the floor; a mixture of soft and hard.

"Loreen?" I call out.

"Up here, Kendall."

At the top of the landing, I see Loreen sitting on the floor cross-legged with candles surrounding her. "Weren't you just walking around?"

She indicates no with her head.

"I heard that," Taylor said. "It sounded like footsteps."

Shelby-Nichole sighs. "I hear that all the time. I'm telling you, it's just best to ignore it."

Celia scowls at our hostess's stepdaughter. "You can't ignore anything when you're investigating. The point is to make a note of everything you see, feel, and/or hear, so you can debunk it or label it as paranormal."

"Oh, sure, I understand." Shelby-Nichole moves into the background and quietly watches.

I slide onto the floor next to Loreen and gaze into her face. She's not in any kind of trance, but she seems watchful of . . . something.

"What are you sensing?"

Loreen twitches her mouth. "I don't want to say. You should come into this with no front-loading."

"What's front-loading?" Taylor asks as she takes a seat next to me.

Celia sits too. "It's having too much knowledge up front about the place you're investigating, to the point where it can cloud your opinions or judgments. That's why I try not to tell Kendall too much about our cases before we get into them."

Everyone comes together in the attic, an we all sit in a circle. Loreen is to my left, Taylor on my right. Next to her is Celia, Becca, Jason, Shelby-Nichole, and Donn. Loreen breaks out the Ovilus, this round electronic disk with two rows of lights up the middle, and sets it on the floor; it's hooked up to a small set of RadioShack speakers that Celia brought. The device clicks on, runs through its start-up and then settles down. Loreen explained to me earlier that we can ask questions of it and it will answer.

"Are there any spirits here with us tonight?" Loreen asks.

The red lights on the Ovilus shine out. "Yes," the computerized voice says.

"How many spirits are here?"

"Girl."

"Who is the girl?" Loreen continues.

"Shunned . . . shunned . . . shunned," the Ovilus says.

Celia's mouth drops open. "I read that it's programmed *not* to repeat words!"

"Shh," Becca says. She holds one of her digital recorders out close to the speaker. "Keep going, Loreen."

"Who was shunned?" she asks.

"Sad."

"Someone was sad?"

"Secret. Sad. Lock."

Taylor snaps a few pictures as Celia continues to take notes. I'm riveted by this little device that picks up on energy around us and translates it into words.

"What lock?" I ask.

"Death. Death. Death."

"There it goes, repeating again," Celia says excitedly.

"Tell us about the lock. Was someone locked up here in this attic?"

"Yes. Lock. Death."

Ugh . . . I wish it would just tell me what I want to know. "Can you be more specific?"

"Secret."

"Who's secret?" Loreen asks.

"Kill. Mother. Now."

The words in the strident, computerized voice chill me.

"Kill. Fall. You."

"Who is you?" I ask.

"You. You. You."

Loreen's gaze touches mine. "I don't like this. I think we should end the investigation."

"No," I beg. "We're getting somewhere with this."

Taylor shudders next to me. "I'm with Loreen. I don't like where this is going."

"Mayor Shy?" Celia asks. "What do you think? Was someone's mother killed in this house?"

She adjusts the bill of her cap. "I don't rightly know. I'm sure that *someone* must have passed on in this house over the many years. Mayer had his attack here before dying at the hospital. Mayer, honey, are you with us?"

"Push. Hurt. Blood."

"Daddy? Is that you?" Shelby-Nichole adds.

"No."

"It's someone else," Loreen confirms. Her face flattens into a grimace and she shudders. Her hands wrap around her upper arms and she rocks back and forth slightly. "I don't like where this is going. Something's not right."

I decide to speak to this spirit like I converse with Emily. In my head, I say, *Whoever you are, if there's anything we can help you with, please let us know. We're not here to harm you. We just want to understand you. My name is Kendall and I'm a psychic. I can feel your pain and hear your voice. You can use me to talk to the rest of the group.*

In my head, I hear Emily gasp. *You shouldn't have said that!*

Ruh-roh. Maybe not the right words.

While Loreen and I have talked a lot about channeling spirits, I've never actually tried to do it. It's not exactly something one can practice. I know that I have to open up and allow a spirit to flow through me, but I've always been too chickenshit to try it. I don't think I have a choice now. Something itches at the back of my neck. A tapping, if you will, of someone wanting to come in. Should I let them? How can I keep them away if I've already said they could use me? I mean, I was talking about, like, whispering in my ear and letting me interpret . . . not . . .

I spread my hands out in front of me and I can . . . see through my fingers like they're made of glass. Whoa! What's happening here? Even though I know I'm sitting, I'm not. I'm standing and backing away from myself into a smoky mist behind me. This is freaky! Suddenly, the sun is shining and the sky is bluer than Jason's eyes ever thought of being. I'm almost floating in the air, over a green mountain covered with kudzu. The peak gives way to a valley filled with yellow and white daffodils, like it's the height of spring. I know it's February here in Radisson, and I didn't think the flowers would bloom this early. Where am I? Am I still in town?

No . . . I'm at the beach. A beautiful white beach. The water is the color of a swimming pool, and the sand looks like grains of sugar. Where is this beach and how did I get here? I touch my toe into the foamy surf and find the water clean and cool to the touch. Slowly, I draw myself into the ocean and sit, feeling the liquid surround me with loving arms, lapping at my bare feet. The smell of salt tickles my nose and I'm hungry for a gigantic seafood dinner. Mmm . . . flounder, scallops, shrimp, and lobster.

Over to the left, a school of dolphins frolic in the water, breaking the surface with their fins and tails as if to welcome me, then diving down into the crystal water. I reach out to the precious babies—okay, they're babies to me—but they're too far away. Their elegance and grace astounds me as I feel my heart pound away in my chest with excitement and glee. This is the most relaxing and happy place I've ever been in my life. There's not a care in the world. I'm safe. I'm secure. But where is here?

Have I died?

Ouch! Who just hit me?

And now with the shaking?

What's going on? Who's . . . ?

"Kendall! Come back to us!" Loreen shouts.

I slowly open my eyes and squint into the flashlight Celia is beaming into my face. "Shit, Celia . . . thanks for blinding me."

"Are you okay, Kendall?" she asks. Her brows are knit together in worry.

Someone's rubbing my forehead, petting me, almost. A big, strong hand. Of course, it's Jason.

He glares down at me, rage steaming off him. "I swear to God, Kendall. Don't you *ever* frickin' do that again!"

CHAPTER TEN

"DON'T DO *WHAT* AGAIN?" I manage to ask, my throat dry and achy.

Celia looks like she's just come off a roller-coaster ride. "Holy crappity-crap, Kendall—you just channeled a spirit!"

Shiitake on a shingle. I did what?

Loreen moves closer. "Are you okay, hon?"

The fog surrounding my brain starts to lift and I feel myself coming out of some sort of trance. Celia's about to smack me again when my eyes pop wide open and connect with hers. "Enough with the abuse," I say with a slight giggle, trying to make light of whatever just happened.

"Are you back, Kendall?" Loreen asks with great distress.

"Did I go somewhere?" Oh, wait . . . wasn't I at the beach? That was merely a dream though . . . wasn't it? I'm obviously going insane once and for all.

"You were channeling, Kendall," Loreen explains to me. "Can you tell me what you remember?"

Jason helps me sit up and I lean into his strong chest as he continues to hold me. I rub my head and try to re-create whatever went on. I tell Loreen and my friends about the peaceful beach and how I floated away.

"I don't remember anything specific other than I just seemed to step back from myself."

"How could you do that, Kendall?" Taylor asks. "You allowed a spirit to take hold of you!"

Jason shakes me. "I'm serious as a heart attack. Don't *ever* pull that again."

"I didn't know I was doing it. I mean, I was talking to the spirit in my head and I guess I sort of gave it permission to use me."

Loreen takes my hand and holds on tightly. "You did it, though, Kendall. You allowed the spirit to control you. I had no idea you were ready for that."

Neither did I. Sweat dots my brow. I feel like I've been rode hard and put away wet. Sorry, horse term I picked up from watching the equestrian dressage during the last Olympics.

What is wrong with me? I just channeled a frickin' dead person!

Celia's still on her knees in front of me waving her hands to fan me. "I want to know all about it. Every single detail."

"I-I was floating . . . it was so peaceful and serene."

Celia rolls her eyes. "That's all you're giving me?"

I explain what I experienced, but I want to know what was happening while I was . . . er . . . away.

Taylor pulls her Sony camcorder from her lap. "I've got it all recorded."

Jason rubs my head. "Are you sure you want to see this? You sort of freaked me the hell out."

Nodding, I slowly move over to where Taylor's seated. She opens up the LCD screen and hits Play.

My eyes grow wide as I watch myself on the video. It's me, yet it's . . . not.

"Kendall! What the hell is going on?" Jason screams on the taping.

On the screen, I slump over and begin to twitch. Then I stop moving. Jason drags me into his lap. Celia is to my right. Taylor zooms the camera in on me.

On the recording, Becca gasps in horror. "Holy shit! Is she okay?"

"She's channeling," Loreen explains from off camera; you can hear her telling everyone to remain calm.

"Why are you here?" I hear myself ask. Okay, well, my mouth moves, but that's so not my voice. It's a scratchy voice, deep, like a whiskey drinker.

"What's going on, Loreen?" I hear Taylor ask. "Can you help her?"

"Kendall's okay. She's stepped away so this spirit can come forward. Who are you?" Loreen asks.

In Jason's arms, I twitch and twist. "Who are *you*?"

"My name is Loreen Woods and these are my friends."

People introduce themselves as I lie there breathing hard. Chunky intakes of air to sustain this spirit overcoming me.

"You know our names. Can you tell me who you are? Are you Mayer Holt?"

"Daddy?" Shelby-Nichole pipes up.

My teeth grit together. "I am no man!"

"What's your name, sugar?" Donn asks so calmly you'd think she is a professional investigator herself.

My eyes shoot open and I'm glaring in Donn's and Loreen's direction. "My name is Sherry. Sherry Biddison. You're in my house. Aiding them."

"Aiding who?" Celia asks.

"Them!"

Loreen is the voice of reason. "Tell us what we can do to help you, Sherry."

"No-no-no one can help me," I growl. Bitterness laces this spirit's every word. "Where were you when they locked me away? Who was here to help me then?"

Celia leans into the frame. "You were locked away? In this house?"

More growling from me. Deep in my chest, like I'm tamping down the pain from this woman. "Treated like chattel. No way to live." I squirm and my eyes close again. "The blond woman who lives in my house will pay for what happened to me. You all will."

"Kendall, what's happening?" There's almost a begging in Jason's voice. "Come back to me!"

The camera wobbles, and the image becomes crooked as everyone moves near me. A melee of voices talking over one another fills the audio; sleeves and arms cover the screen. This is when Jason and Celia start yelling at me, while Celia smacks the ever-loving boogink (my Grandma Ethel's word for *shit*) out of me. Ouch!

"Whoa," I say when I'm done watching the video.

"Do you remember any of that?" Taylor asks.

"Nope. *Nada.* Zilch."

Mayor Shy gnaws on her bottom lip. "What did this Sherry Biddison mean about my paying for what happened to her? Does she think I'm responsible?"

Loreen wrings her hands together. "That's probably why you've been having these body aches. This Biddison woman is attached to your house and is uneasy with the living."

Shelby-Nichole clears her throat. "I wonder if this is the woman I've seen."

Celia's attention spins to Shelby-Nichole, as does Donn's. "You've *seen* her, sugar?" the mayor asks her stepdaughter.

The girl's eyes fill with tears behind her glasses. She tugs them off and dabs at her face with the back of her hand. "I've tried to ignore it 'cause I didn't want to admit anything was there. But yeah . . . I've seen a woman."

"Do you think you could describe her to Celia? She can draw amazing pictures based on descriptions," I say.

"Let's do it," Celia says.

"Right now?"

"No better time," Celia tells Shelby-Nichole.

The two of them go off into another room to work on

the drawing. Becca threads her headphones over her ears and starts reviewing her EVPs. Taylor excuses herself to go outside and get some air. If I had the strength to follow her, I would. Instead, I stretch my arms in front of me for a hand up.

Loreen and Jason help me to my unsteady feet, and Donn wraps her arm around me. "Can I get you some water?"

"Yes, ma'am. That would be nice."

When the mayor leaves the room, I move to a nearby couch and collapse into the bulky cushions. I let out a long sigh. "I can't believe what I just watched. That was really me!"

"You certainly surprised me," Loreen says with a grin.

"To say the least," Jason snaps.

I twist around to face him. "What's eating you?"

His handsome face falls. "How can I protect you, Kendall, when you go and do something so asinine?"

"I've told you I don't need protection, Jason. You have enough to worry about with your sister and mom and all that stuff."

"Kendall, I—"

I stop him with my hand. "There is a very bitter spirit in this house that is causing the occupants suffering. Shelby-Nichole is afraid to acknowledge what she's seen and heard. Donn has intense back and shoulder pain from this Biddison woman. I can't just walk away. We've got to do a lot of research and find out who she is, and I've got to get her to cross into the light."

She doesn't want to go . . .

Emily appears across the room.

"What do you mean, she doesn't want to go?"

Loreen and Jason look around, both realizing at the same moment that I'm speaking to my spirit guide.

"You're treading on dangerous ground."

"How so, Emily?"

"What's she saying?" Jason asks.

"Emily wants me to stay away from this spirit."

He sits next to me and takes my hand. "Then listen to her."

I put my hand on my chest. "I just, like, became one with this spirit. I let her use me to speak to you guys. I can't simply abandon this investigation."

"What about your vision?" Jason asks, his eyes shining with apprehension.

I bite my lower lip slightly. "It's only that, Jason. You and Emily are so overprotective of me. It's like I can't go to the bathroom without one of you thinking my vision is going to come true. I'm already scared of my own shadow. What more do you want me to do? Lock myself away in my house, like what was apparently done to Sherry Biddison?"

"Kendall . . ." Jason inhales deeply, his chest rising and then falling in a most dramatic manner. "I've dreamed about you too."

"Awww . . . how sweet," I say with a smile.

He blushes slightly. "Not like that. Bad dreams."

"Of something horrible happening to me?"

There's an eight-months-pregnant pause. Then he breathes, "Yeah."

I smile as best as I can, considering my pulse is jetting away under my skin. "You've been watching too many late-night movies on On Demand."

His blue eyes darken. "I'm serious, Kendall. I can't shake this. We're connected, you and me. I love you and I want to protect you at all costs."

"So now we're sharing dreams?"

He shrugs. "Seems like it."

Geez Louise! Does that mean he's also seen the images of the guy with the gray hair? God, Jason's going to think I'm cheating on him in my dreams.

Donn returns and hands me a large glass of ice water. I reach for it and begin gulping it down to quench the fire inside me. I don't know if it's residual energy from my connection with Sherry Biddison or the fear that something looms in my future that could severely alter my life.

Jason sits back on the couch and runs his hands through his hair. Loreen hitches her hip onto the arm of the sofa and gazes down at me. "You're full of anxiety."

"Damn right I am," I say, like it's the understatement of the year.

Loreen's voice is as soothing as a warm bubble bath. "Have faith, Kendall. God has a path for you. Follow your life purpose."

"Even if it means putting myself in harm's way?"

"We can't live every moment in fear."

"Yeah, we can," Jason points out.

Loreen stretches out her hand. "We're all in this together. You, me, your team, Donn, and Shelby-Nichole. We'll get to the bottom of this. There's research to be done on Sherry Biddison so we'll know how to handle her the next time. We'll keep you safe, help this spirit, and make sure this house is clean. It's what we're meant to do."

I really hope she's right.

CHAPTER ELEVEN

CELIA BOUNDS TOWARD ME in the hallway at school Monday morning, waving some sort of printout in my face. "You'll never believe what I've got."

"Info on Sherry Biddison?" I've been thinking about the spirit nonstop since our investigation on Saturday.

Stopping in her tracks, Celia frowns. "No. I mean, sort of, but no. I have something on Emily."

Jesus in the garden! With all my thoughts of Sherry, I'd forgotten that my spirit guide is Emily Faulkner with a Wisconsin license plate. "Whatcha got?"

"Would you believe there are actually *four* missing persons named Emily Faulkner? Paul found files from Illinois, Kentucky, Indiana, and Ohio."

"That many?"

She bobs her head in excitement. "See, the thing is, even though we know the plate you saw in your vision was registered to Emily Faulkner, records in Wisconsin couldn't locate the actual car. I bet what happened was that since the car caught fire, all traces of it were destroyed, to the point that it was demolished or recycled or what have you."

"Like the plate melted in the wreck?"

"Yeah, something like that."

"So even though the car was registered to Emily Faulkner, there's no proof of what I saw happen to the car?" I ask, trying to grasp this info.

"Right. See here." Celia shows me the report her cousin faxed to her. "He's also cross-referencing the hospitals in these four states to see if there were any Jane Does that showed up in any of the ERs pregnant or with a deceased baby."

I rub my temples. Right—Emily's baby. What in the world happened to the baby? I wish my psychic abilities could help me figure this out. "Isn't that a lot of searching?"

Celia dismissed the thought. "That's what computers are for. They do all the work on the data." She lays a hand on my arm. "We're going to find out who she is and where she came from, Kendall."

I smile at my friend. "I appreciate all you're doing, Celia. It is important for me to know Emily's backstory and why she's attached to me. However, I'm going to focus on Sherry Biddison while we're waiting for the research from your cousin. There's something desperate about her situation, the way she's wreaking havoc on Donn and Shelby-Nichole. Besides, I can't get Sherry out of my mind. Especially since she's actually hurting Mayor Shy. I had seen Sherry through the windows there even before I knew anything about her. She's out for vengeance."

Celia's eyes drop to her feet and she kicks her sneakered feet against my locker. Her black hair falls in her face, and I can see something is bothering her. It's damn near written in Sharpie across her forehead.

"What?"

"Nothing."

"Celia . . ."

"It's okay, Kendall. Really."

I focus my attention on Celia, reaching out to her psychically. I break through the mental barriers my friend has put up to see deep into her thoughts. I sigh when I catch a glimpse of what's troubling her. "Oh, Celia. You're upset because throughout all of our investigations and ghost hunting, *you* haven't had a real paranormal experience. That's not true at all. What about the EVPs we've captured? And the ectoplasm photographs? And my channeling the other night?"

Her eyes connect with mine. "That's all shit that's happened to you. I mean, sure, we get EVPs and some cool photos. But I've never *seen* anything. I can't see Emily. I can't hear who you talk to, and I'm not a vessel for channeling or anything. It's frustrating as hell."

Bless her heart. I wish I could manifest an apparition for her. "You'll see something when the time is right, Celia."

"When?"

"When you least expect it."

She waves me off with the flick of her wrist. "Are you telling me to be patient? 'Cause I ain't patient," she says snarkily. "I'm anything but patient."

With a laugh, I say, "Look, I'll promise you something, Celia. If I die before you, I will totally come back and show myself to you."

"Seriously?"

"Yeah . . . like when I'm ninety-five and you're barely getting around in your walker in the old folks home." I crack myself up at the thought of Celia and me being blue-haired little old ladies.

This makes her smile. "You'd better do it, Moorehead."

I hope it's a *loooooooooong* time before I have to make good on this promise.

Monday after school, Mom walks into the kitchen, her face unusually pale. Oh God, she's not expecting, is she? No . . . no, this isn't about my family. It's about the Tillsons.

Taylor glances up from the French homework she's got scattered over the table. "What is it, Miss Sarah?"

A large man steps into the room behind Mom and slowly removes his aviator sunglasses. Taylor's breath catches when she sees him. Although they're not the clear blue eyes I'm used to gazing into, I know for a fact that this is Jason and Taylor's father. His hair is clipped close to his head. His skin is remarkably tan considering he lives in the Last Frontier. He's wearing worn jeans and a brown leather jacket that's seen better days.

"Hey, baby girl," he says to Taylor.

She sits up straight and moves her long hair off her shoulders. "Daddy," she says with no emotion in her voice. "What are you doing here?"

Mr. Tillson moves farther into the room and spreads his arms open for his daughter. Taylor doesn't react. Instead, she begins stacking up her French book and notebook. He slices his eyes over to my mother, who frowns at the icy interaction.

"I'm here for you and Jason, sweetie," he says.

"About time," Taylor mutters so low that only I can hear her. Taylor lifts her eyes briefly. "I see."

Great googly-moogly. The tension is a thickening agent you could make gravy out of. Needing to help out, I push to my feet and extend my right hand to the man who fathered my boyfriend. "Hey, Mr. Tillson. I'm Kendall."

He politely takes my hand in his larger one and pumps up and down. "Pleasure, Kendall. I've heard a lot of good things about you from Jason."

Slipping into the role of Southern hostess, Mom begins to fuss over her guests. "Here, Russ." She motions to the armchair in the corner. "Please have a seat. What can I get you? Coffee? A soda pop, maybe? Or some sweet tea?"

He smiles weakly—not at Mom but over his disappointment in his daughter—and says, "Tea would be great, Sarah. Thanks." Russ Tillson lowers his six-foot frame into the chair and leans forward, his hands on his knees. "So, no hug for your old man, Taylor?"

She wets her lips quickly and shrugs her shoulders. "I think I've grown out of that, Daddy."

Mom nearly shoves the glass of iced tea at Mr. Tillson. "Here you go. Taylor? Anything for you, dear?"

"No, ma'am, *merci*."

The front doorbell sounds out. Mom turns to get it. A moment later, Russ Tillson's younger doppelgänger enters the room. Unlike his sister, Jason goes to hug his father, who stands when his son enters the room. It's quick contact. Sort of like football players who do the obligatory team chest bump and stuff when they score. Taylor knits her brows together and sighs.

"Good to see you, son," Mr. Tillson says. He ruffles Jason's shaggy blond mess. "You need a haircut."

Jason sloughs off the comment. "Whatever. When did you get in?"

"Really late last night. I didn't want to bother you kids, knowing you had school today. So I went to the hospital and stayed with your mom."

"How is she?" I ask, knowing Taylor wanted to inquire about Rachel Tillson's status today.

"Maybe you'd like to go into the living room," Mom suggests. "So you can have some privacy with your children."

Taylor balks, though. "It doesn't matter, Miss Sarah. We can stay right here. Besides, Kendall's psychic, so either she'll figure it out or Jason will share the information with her. We might as well all stay right here."

There's so much pain in her beautiful face. The resentment toward her father emanates from her like heat from the pavement on a hot summer day. I close my eyes momentarily and take a deep breath. I send some Reiki energy to her and add a quick prayer asking God to open her ears and heart to her father, who has traveled so far to be with her, despite the problems he and his wife are going through. Whether she knows it or not, Taylor needs her dad.

"Very well, then," Mr. Tillson says. He drains the iced tea and returns the glass to the kitchen counter. "Jason, sit, son."

Jason obeys, pulling me to his side and taking my hand. I squeeze his fingers to let him know I'm here for him— anything he needs.

With an awkward throat clear, Mr. Tillson says, "Kids, your mom has taken a turn for the worse."

Taylor's eyes immediately become glassy with fresh tears. "Wh-wh-what's wrong now? I saw her last night and she was getting better. We watched CNN together."

Mom crosses the room and places her hand on Taylor's trembling shoulder for support. My friend reaches out for comfort.

Mr. Tillson continues. "Her vitals are good and her blood pressure has leveled out. However, she's still slipping into unconsciousness for extended periods of time and that has the doctors quite concerned. It seems that the combination of pills she took was quite powerful, and the doctors can't be sure at this point of the extent of her neurological damage. She'll need a lot more tests and more than likely some serious rehabilitation, almost as if she's a stroke victim."

"Oh, Mom . . ." Taylor no longer holds back her sobs. My mom hands her a checkered napkin from the basket on the lazy Susan to help out.

A tremor travels through Jason, vibrating my hand. "What does that mean?"

"It means that we're going to have to find a place to move her."

"Move her? Where?" Taylor asks.

Mr. Tillson sighs hard. "An institution, possibly."

Taylor bolts up. "You can't have my mama institutionalized! I won't let you!"

"Taylor, would you just calm down and—"

"No, Dad! I won't." Her eyes darken and dilate as her unusual fury boils over. She grabs her homework and crams it into her backpack. "You haven't been here. You don't know. You left us. And now you want to take her away from us?"

"Sweetie, I don't want to take her away—"

"Taylor, quit acting like a baby," Jason says.

"Stop telling me what to do. I have yearbook stuff to work on. I'll be at school." She storms out the door.

"Let her go," their father says. "She needs time."

Jason rubs his head. "Whatever. Drama queen."

I elbow him hard. "She's dealing with this the only way she knows how. Be nice."

His eyes soften and he nods. "Sorry."

Russ Tillson addresses my mom. "Sarah, if you and David don't mind looking after Taylor for a few more days, I would appreciate it. I need to talk to the doctors and check with our insurance to see what arrangements can be made to make Rachel comfortable for as long as necessary."

"Of course, Russ," Mom states. "We consider Taylor family. Anything you need." She turns to my boyfriend. "You too, Jason."

"Thanks, Miss Sarah," he says politely.

Taylor needs me now more than ever, so I reach for my purse and excuse myself. "I should go see what I can do to help with the yearbook too."

Jason is well aware that I'm following after Taylor. He kisses me on the head to thank me.

"Stay and talk to your dad," I whisper.

"I will."

"I'll take care of Tay."

I slip out to my car and head in the direction of RHS. As much as Taylor's been here for me through my awakening and dealings with Courtney Langdon last semester when she was jealous of my psychic abilities, I'm here for her now.

It's not every day that a girl stands to lose her mother . . . forever.

Two days later, everything changes.

I'm at Loreen's store after a successful afternoon going around the Radisson Square stores hawking ads for the

Rambler with Shelby-Nichole—scored seven ads, thankyou-verymuch!—when a sallow-faced Taylor tromps in with news that rocks my world.

And not in a good way.

"I'm moving to freaking Alaska."

I hear the words leave her mouth, but I don't believe what she's saying.

"You're . . . what?" Shelby-Nichole says, voicing my own surprise. "We can't lose you on yearbook!"

I eyeball her. "Not the time . . ."

Shelby-Nichole winces and steps aside.

Taylor collapses to the couch and puts her head in her hands. I'm unsure exactly how to spin this. She might as well tell me that she's moving to Mongolia, or the moon.

"And Jason too?"

Her nod is like a bullet to my chest.

She lifts her eyes and sadness outlines her pretty face. "Dad talked to my Aunt Pamela, Mom's sister. They're moving my mom into a home north of Atlanta to monitor her. Dad talked to his lawyer and is filing an injunction for temporary custody of Jason and me while Mom is incapacitated."

"Does Jason know this?" I ask, my mouth arid as the Mojave Desert.

"Oh, yeah. He's heartbroken," she says. "He disappeared. No idea where he is."

I touch my fingers to the hematite bracelet Jason gave me. The one that is exactly like the one I gave him. The stones are smooth, yet cold to my touch. They sing a vibration to my soul, and for some unknown reason, I know where my guy is.

I reach for my car keys. "I'll find him."

Tears pour from Taylor's eyes, and Shelby-Nichole moves to comfort her. "I'm just a kid. I shouldn't have to deal with this. It's not fair. To leave school, my friends, the ghost hunting, the yearbook . . . and Ryan." She sniffs hard and runs her fist underneath her nose.

"We'll dedicate the *Rambler* to you, Taylor," Shelby-Nichole says, trying to help.

Taylor smiles, then purses her lips into a pout. "I'm so not trying to be a tart about this, but this is all Mom's fault! Why did she have to do what she did? It was so selfish. And it's ruining everything for Jason and me." She sniffles again. "I had plans. A life course. A curriculum I was following for my future. What am I going to do in Alaska? Catch salmon? Chip ice? Duke will never admit me now."

Shelby-Nichole holds her tighter. "Oh, sweetie. Don't think like that."

I have no idea how to make this better for anyone. Still, I say, "Your mom obviously had a lot of issues that she needed to sort out. Therapy isn't always enough for some people. But her weakness in attempting to take her own life doesn't reflect on you, Taylor. And it doesn't have to alter your life plan, either. You're smart and talented and beautiful, and no matter where you end up, your future is bright." Hello, when did Dr. Phil walk in the room? Maybe I'm channeling *him* now. Oy vey!

Taylor smirks at me through her tears. "You're such a grownup sometimes."

"Yeah, well . . . comes with the territory of being psychic and knowing everyone's business."

"Why don't I drive you over to the hospital," Shelby-Nichole offers to Taylor.

"That's a good idea," I chime in. I wink at Shelby-Nichole and she smiles back.

I have to get to Jason.

And for once, I am connected psychically to him. His heart is heavy with doubt and sorrow. But mostly, he's concerned about . . . leaving me.

I pull my Fit into the empty parking lot of Town Lake. Well, empty save for a black Jeep. Jason's Jeep. He's sitting at the end of the short pier bouncing a fishing pole in the murky green water.

"Practicing for life in Alaska?" I ask, trying to lighten the air.

He squints into the sun to see me. "I guess you've heard, huh?"

"Yeah, Taylor's beside herself."

Jason fidgets with the lure, reeling it in and then tossing it back out twenty feet in front of him. "She's not the only one."

He turns to me and slides his hand against my cheek. I rub into it much like Eleanor, Buckley, and Natalie do when it's dinnertime and they give thanks against my calf muscle.

"I don't want to leave you, Kendall," Jason says softly.

I kiss him tenderly. "I don't want you to either, but what can you do?"

"I told Dad that I could live with Roachie so I can finish school. He won't have it, though. Says I'm too young to be on my own."

I thread my fingers through the fingers of his left hand. "Well, you are."

Jason pulls away. "I can take care of myself. I've been doing it since he left for Alaska to start with. Now he wants to drag me into his world."

I gaze into his troubled eyes. I have no earthly clue what to say to him. Instead, I clink our hematite bracelets together; the magnets reach out to each other. "We'll always be together, Jason. Distance is nothing for us. We can e-mail and call and visit each other."

"You know that's not going to happen. You're going to move on. You'll forget me. Hell, maybe I should forget you."

Ummm . . . hold the phone! What did he just say?

The hairs on the back of my neck rise up. "*Excuse* me?"

Jason drops my hand and wipes his palm against his jeans as if my touch were poisonous. "Ever since you came into my life, nothing has been the same. Instead of concentrating on taking care of Mom and Taylor, I've been worrying about you."

"Wait just a damn minute now—"

He points his index finger in my face. "No! You wait! You've possessed me, Kendall Moorehead. With your psychic awakening and ghost hunting and being so different from the other girls here in Radisson. I don't know what you've done, but all I think about is you and if you're all right or in danger. You! To the detriment of my own family. Taylor's changed right before my eyes, and Mom . . . well, Mom's a friggin' mess!"

"Jason! This isn't my—"

He stands now, pacing on the pier. "If I hadn't been so consumed with you, with the dreams I constantly have about something hurting you, I would have been there for my mom. I could take better care of my sister. I could keep my family together and not have to move to freakin' Alaska with the moose and polar bears!"

I stand too and fist my hands at my sides. "How *dare* you, Jason Tillson! I come here to tell you how much I love you and will miss you and how we can keep in touch, and you try to lay this all on me?" I want to cry, but the tears just won't form yet. I think my tear ducts are as horrified as I am.

Jason's not himself. Not at all. But what do I expect, considering the turn of events? Still, he lashes out at me. "I can't get you out of my head, Kendall. I think it's love, but mostly it's this obsession with keeping you safe. I, too, have dreams of you hurt and dying. And I can't stop it." He pounds his chest. "Do you know what kind of responsibility that is? I can't help my sister, I couldn't help my mom, so how the hell am I supposed to help you?"

"Jason, nothing's going to—"

"You don't know that, K!"

No, I don't know that. He's right.

His hands return to his hair and he scrubs at his scalp. "I can't explain any of this. Just that you've been a distraction."

"We're connected, Jason. Cosmically. We were meant to be together." I know this with every fiber of my being.

"God, you're just losing it now," he says. "Everyone is. I can't save everyone."

I put my hand on his arm. "No one is asking you to. Especially not me."

A smirk crosses his face. "Oh, that's just great. Go out there and channel unknown spirits and flop around the floor like a fish out of the tank. Right. That's healthy. That's normal."

I nearly growl. "It's normal for *me* and you know that!"

He stops for a minute, his chest rising and falling emphatically with every breath. Then he musters up more verbal ammunition. "I forbid you to ghost hunt anymore."

I have to laugh. A bubble of near-psychotic amusement pops out of me. "I don't *think* so!"

"Seriously, Kendall. If I'm gone to Alaska and not here to protect you, then I don't want you ghost hunting anymore."

Hands on hips, I step back. "That's absurd, Jason. You know this is my calling."

"Then don't answer the phone," he says sarcastically.

I know he's only lashing out at me because of everything going on, but damnit, he's pissing me off big-time. The strong-willed little animal inside of me rears up on its hind legs, and I feel myself about to give the I Am Woman, Hear Me Roar speech.

"I'll do whatever I want, Jason!" I grit my teeth to try and temper my rage. "You think you're the only person who's had anything happen to him? Remember, I was ripped out of the home I've known my entire life in Chicago to be dragged down here to Where Jesus Lost His Sandals, Georgia, where I have been teased, ridiculed, poked fun at, mistreated, ostracized, and cast out. Yeah, shit happens, but we deal with it. It is what it is. You can't control other people's lives, though. Your mom is responsible for herself, as is Taylor, as am I."

His lips flatten. "So you're going to defy me?"

"Is your name David Moorehead?" I smart off. "Last time I checked, he's still got the job of Kendall's father."

Jason bends down and snags his car keys and fishing gear. "Fine. If you want to continue to put yourself at risk and ghost hunt, then go ahead. I wash my hands of you."

"What's that supposed to mean?"

Fire blazes in his eyes. "You're on your own from here on out, Kendall."

"Fine!"

"Fine!"

And with that, the love of my life turns and storms away.

When his Jeep is out of sight, I collapse to the pier and cry.

Chapter Twelve

THE REST OF THIS WEEK sucks ass.

Taylor's in a funk.

Jason's in a funk.

I'm in a funk.

Celia and Becca are in a funk 'cause the rest of us are so funky with one another. It's a total cluster—well, you know the rest of the word.

Friday at lunch, Becca opts to let a Trance CD play while she sits at the lunch table with Celia and me. Celia's knee-deep in her research of Sherry Biddison, as well as her continued study on everything Emily Faulkner. Her cousin Paul is still sifting through missing-persons reports to get us some information. Interestingly, Emily has made herself very scarce. She knows we're digging into her past and apparently wants nothing to do with it. Great—*now* she leaves me alone.

Becca opens a pack of Twix, removes one, and slides the other one across the table to me. "You need some medication, g'friend."

I smile, take the offered chocolate, and crunch down into

it. Mmmm . . . Woman's best friend—despite Marilyn thinking it's diamonds.

"Thanks, Dr. Asiaf."

I'm finishing up the sugary treat—and licking every last morsel off my fingers—when Shelby-Nichole plops down next to me.

"Y'all . . . I need help." Her face is flushed and she's visibly shaking. "I got to school late today, but I've been wanting to talk to y'all."

"What's going on?" I ask.

"Something's terribly wrong with Donn," Shelby-Nichole says, her voice low.

"Why are you whispering?" Becca asks.

Stunned, Shelby-Nichole says, "Because she's, like, the mayor of the entire town. It doesn't bode well for Radisson if she's . . . gone all wack."

I hold my hands up. "Now wait a sec. Tell us what's going on."

Celia removes a notebook from her backpack. "Don't leave out any details."

Shelby-Nichole steadies herself. "Last night, I was watching TV in my room and I heard screaming. Loud screaming. I bolted from my room with my typing trophy in my hand as a weapon. I found Donn sitting at the base of the grand staircase, her knees pulled up to her chin, and she was rocking back and forth."

"Yowza," Becca comments. "That sounds crazy."

"I know, right?" Shelby-Nichole says. She continues, "Then she starts humming. Not any tune I've ever heard. I can't even explain it other than to say it was eerie and sad. And to top it all off, it wasn't Donn's voice at all."

"Whose voice was it?" Celia asks.

Shelby-Nichole adjusts her glasses. "I don't have the slightest clue, but it wasn't my stepmom."

"Does the city council know this?" Celia asks.

Shelby-Nichole frowns. "Why would I tell them? And have Donn lose her job? Like—no. I'm telling y'all."

"It's Sherry Biddison," I say confidently. "She's trying to run Donn out of the house."

"Who *is* this woman?" Shelby-Nichole asks with heated frustration.

Celia shuffles through her notebook and begins reading us some of the research she's done on the Radisson mayor's mansion. "Back after the Civil War, there was a mayor named Harlan Biddison. His wife was Sherry and they had one son, Harlan Jr.; he married a woman named Virgilian Martin from Pennsylvania, who had nursed him when he was in a Union hospital following the Battle of Gettysburg. There's not much about the family other than Harlan Biddison was the mayor for fourteen years, and then his son, Harlan Jr. was the mayor for ten more." Celia shows me a printout of a portrait of the Biddison family. Harlan has a rather long mustache and beard, and his son is the spitting image of him. The women are a tad bit dowdy in their plain woolen clothing. One woman is standing on each side of the seated men. One is young, with lovely golden curls and a kind face. The other is older, more worn, and bitterness details her face. It's the same woman I saw peeking through the curtain of the mayor's mansion.

I point my finger at the picture. "That is Sherry Biddison."

Celia's brow lifts. "You sure?"

"Yep. I've seen her."

"That's the woman you allegedly channeled," Becca notes. "I got several EVPs from that night. Here." She withdraws a digital voice recorder from the pocket of her jeans and cues up a recording. We all lean over to listen closely.

You can hear me talking as I am channeling the spirit. However, there's also a laced-in voice pattern that's barely whispered.

"Right there," Becca says and hits Rewind. "Listen."

There's static and muffled voices and then, "Killlllllllll her."

"Whoa!" Shelby-Nichole's hand flies to her mouth. "Kill my stepmom?"

"It's not clear," Celia notes. "Could be anyone."

A sigh escapes my chest. "I wish I had more to go on. Something of Sherry Biddison that gives me a better picture of her as a person. All I know is what I've seen. She seems hateful and vengeful against . . . someone."

"Maybe this'll help." Shelby-Nichole reaches into her purse and withdraws a gold pocket watch attached to a long chain. She places it in my hand and explains. "This was my dad's. It was passed on to him by the guy he replaced as mayor. Supposedly, this dates back to the early 1800s and was used by every mayor of the city. Donn didn't feel right taking it, so she passed it along to me. I carry it with me as a reminder of him. Maybe Harlan and Harlan Jr. used it?"

"Let's see what residual energy is attached to this." I flip the timepiece over in my palm as I breathe deeply. Flashed images of family dinners. Discussions of politics and America's future. Who to appoint as city clerk. The golden-haired woman working on mending. Servants tending to the lawn and garden. "I'm getting a lot of arguments. Raised voices. Disagreements. Men who weren't sure in what direction to take the city of Radisson after the war. Resentment over Yankees and carpet-baggers moving into town." I tighten my eyes and continue to filter the visions. Sherry's image comes into view. Her teeth are clenched. Deep lines are drawn across her once attractive face. The years of war and turmoil have caught up with her. A bitter taste forms in my mouth from the hatred filling Sherry Biddison's soul. There is severe hatred for . . . Virgilian and the baby she carries. Sherry has a plan.

My eyelids flutter open and I focus on the friends before me. "We have to get in there and finish our investigation. I know why Sherry's still here, and we have to make her cross into the light before she hurts the mayor." I glance at Shelby-Nichole. "Or you . . . or anyone."

Right now, I have no worry about my own physical well-being. I'm not scared of what my visions may have predicted about the future. I'm ignoring Emily's warnings to stay out of this case. I'm brushing aside Jason's concern. This is who I am and what I do. I'm a ghost huntress and I have to help this spirit.

"Who's up for a ghost hunt?" I ask.

"I'm in," Becca says quickly.

Celia winks. "You know I am."

Shelby-Nichole takes the watch back from me. "I'd like to help."

"Of course," I say with a warm smile to my new friend. "And we'll need one more person."

I nab my BlackBerry from my pocket and hit #4 on the speed dial. When the sweet, Southern voice answers on the second ring, I say, "Taylor Tillson. Hey, hon. I know you're packing up to leave, but we've got one more investigation before you head to Alaska. We can't do this without you."

I can sense her smile radiating through the phone. "What time do we start?"

"My dad isn't happy that I'm doing this," Taylor whispers. We're sitting in the darkened living room of Donn Shy, waiting.

"Did you tell him what this is all about?" I ask.

She nods. "*Oui.* He isn't too keen on this as an after-school activity. Especially when Jason gets like he's been lately. What did you two fight about?"

I swallow the lump in my throat at the mention of his

name. We haven't talked since that day on the pier. No phone calls. No texts. Nothing. Emily showed up yesterday to criticize him, but I wouldn't listen. It's bad enough that he's leaving town. I hate that things with us are ending on this note.

Fingering the hematite bracelet on my left wrist, I say, "I don't really want to talk about it right now. Not while we're investigating."

"I understand." She sighs hard. "I'm going to miss this. Miss y'all. Miss Ryan."

I pat her leg. "I know, Taylor. It won't be the same around here without you."

A flashlight brightens the room and I glance up to see Celia and Shelby-Nichole joining us. "Y'all getting anything in here?" Celia asks.

"Taylor's gotten a few orbs," I say. "Probably not anything more than dust or bugs."

Shelby-Nichole snickers. "I can assure you there are no bugs in this house."

"Where's Becca?" I ask.

Celia points upward. "At the top of the stairs doing an EVP session with Loreen. Loreen said she was feeling a lot of energy in that hallway, so they camped out there."

"Okay . . . sure."

Celia whispers to me. "My cousin may have a lead on our Emily Faulkner. The Jane Does that fit Emily's description and, er, status—meaning pregnant—were located at Riverside Methodist Hospital in Columbus, Ohio; Marion General

Hospital in Marion, Indiana; and Northwestern Hospital in Chicago, of all places."

The hairs on the back of my neck stand up. "That's where Mom used to work."

"No shit?" Celia asks.

"I shit you not. I wonder if she remembers a pregnant Jane Doe."

"Come on, Kendall. I'm sure your mom has had plenty of Jane Does in her nursing career. You think she'd remember Emily?"

"I don't know. You can bet I'll ask, though."

Donn interrupts us to escort Father Massimo into the room.

"How's it going, ghost huntresses?" he asks with a vibrant smile. "Where's Jason?"

My face falls. "He told me he doesn't want to investigate anymore."

Father Mass winks at me as if to say everything will be okay.

"Is that you, Massimo?" Loreen calls down.

"Yeah, hon."

Hon? They're at the calling-each-other-hon stage?

"Bring the girls up here," she says. "We're getting all kinds of spikes on the EMF detector, and the Ovilus is saying some pretty wild things."

Everyone gathers in the vestibule at the top of the stairs landing. We're surrounded by the finest ghost-hunting equipment, all gathered thanks to Celia's AmEx account from her megarich Mega-Mart parents. To my left is a trifield meter measuring electrical static and radio frequencies. Celia's holding a K-II meter, and Becca's working with two digital voice recorders. Loreen is focusing on the Ovilus—whose creepy computer voice completely icks me out—and Taylor's got infrared cameras placed strategically and is using a couple of handheld video recorders. A laptop sits off to the side measuring the barometric pressure as well as any temperature changes. We are state-of-the-art here. No messing around.

However, after an hour of no hits on any of the machines, Shelby-Nichole lets out a long, loud yawn.

"Sorry, y'all," she says. She takes out her iPhone and scrolls through missed messages. "Damn, Colton called. Hope everything's all right with the *Rambler*. He is working on some layout this weekend. This is kind of boring. Maybe I should go help him."

"At midnight thirty?" Becca says with a bit of a laugh.

"Concentrate, Shelby-Nichole," Taylor instructs like a seasoned pro. "If ghost hunting were easy, everyone would be doing it."

"Truer words were never said," Celia quips.

Loreen suggests that I take out my rose quartz pendulum and try dowsing to see if that helps us make contact with Sherry Biddison.

"Good idea." I draw the crystal in its velvet pouch from my jeans pocket. I run through the normal test of "what is my yes" and "what is my no" to make sure the pendulum and I are connecting to each other.

I focus my energies on the task at hand. "Are there any spirits here with us tonight?"

The rose quartz begins to dance, spinning counterclockwise, which is my indication of yes.

"Is there more than one spirit here?"

The answer spins to no.

"Is the spirit of Sherry Biddison here?" I ask, watching the pendulum intently.

"That's your yes, right?" Celia asks.

I nod.

Taylor starts snapping pictures all around us with her digital camera.

"Sherry, my name is Kendall. We met the last time I was here." I gulp down the knot of foreboding in my throat. I keep reminding myself that I'm a professional and this investigation is no different from the dozens before it, visions, dreams, warnings, and expectations aside. I'm a psychic and I *have* to help this family by crossing Sherry Biddison into the light.

"Sherry," I begin. "Can you please talk to me?"

"I've got a hit on the DVR," Becca says.

When Becca rewinds and hits Play, I hear hissing and crackling and the distinctive whisper of a disembodied voice saying, "I puuuusssssssh you next."

"Holy crap!" Celia exclaims. "Roll that back."

We listen a few more times and, sure enough, the threat of "I push you next" sounds out to us.

I fist the pendulum and lift up to my knees. Ahead, near

the railing, in front of the antique Tiffany hurricane lamp that sits on a maple bureau, I see the formation of a mist. I motion with my head to the area, and Celia is on it, scanning with her meter.

"The needle's buried at ten-plus milligauss," Celia reports.

Taylor's mouth falls open. "That's, like, wicked high, right?"

I stand and take a few deep breaths for courage. "Sherry Biddison—are you here?"

Loreen tugs on the jean fabric of my left knee. "Proceed with caution, Kendall."

Another nod from me.

The wispy mist begins to take shape: a head . . . an arm . . . a wide skirt. Tentatively, I walk forward, as if I'm preparing to pet a wild animal. Sherry Biddison may be as volatile

Unexpectedly, I hear Jason's voice in my head. I don't know if it's really him or merely my memory of him. Whatever the case, the words are distinctive: *You're on your own.*

Yes, I am. Emily's disappeared, Jason's walked away, and no one else can see, feel, or experience what I do, so it's up to me to face off against Sherry.

After I take about eight steps, I halt. I spread my arms wide and toss my head back a bit. "Sherry Biddison, this is no longer your house. You are hurting the occupants—Donn and Shelby-Nichole. You're terrorizing the help and causing them to leave their jobs. Why are you doing this?" The mist shifts and dives around, swirling at my feet before forming into the shape of a woman. "That's you, isn't it, Sherry? Please talk to me. I can help you."

A boom as deafening as thunder roars out. I clasp my hands over my ears and recoil.

"Gooooooooo away! I rid this house of you once. I'll do it again."

"Sherry, I don't know what you're talking about."

Loreen moves behind me. "She's here, Kendall. I can sense her. Be careful."

"Do you want to use me again, Sherry? Do you want me to channel your spirit? Or will you just talk to me? Tell me what's bothering you and let me know how I can help you cross into the light."

The voice bellows out once more. "You're no good for him."

"For who?"

I spin to the left and right, trying to make out the ghostly apparition. The figure sharpens into focus as I squint at the darkness. Moonlight streams in from the nearby window, illuminating the anticipation on the faces of my team. I can see that Celia, especially, wants to see Sherry Biddison for herself.

So do I, for that matter.

And I get my wish. Standing one foot in front of me at the top of the stairs is an older woman, haggard with time and hatred and a war gone wrong. Her hands tightly grip the sides of her gray skirt. Her hair is neatly bunned and pinned, yet the intense fire in her eyes is anything but ladylike or in the vein of true Southern hospitality.

"Let me help you, Sherry."

She speaks through cracked lips and aged teeth. "No one can help me."

"I can. My friends can as well."

She tsk-tsks at me, as much as a dead person can. "It all went wrong. Nothing can change what happened to me."

My pulse accelerates under my skin, itching at me like a case of poison ivy. I tamp down the dread threatening to erode my skill as a psychic. My tongue dashes out to wet my dry lips. "What happened to you, Sherry?"

The ghost growls and moves forward, hands in the air like misty claws bent on swooping down and maiming me. "Wouldn't you like to know?"

A gusty breeze blows me back into my group. Taylor screams. Celia yelps. Becca tugs off her headphones and says, "What the frig was that?"

I catch my breath. "We're about to find out."

CHAPTER THIRTEEN

THE GHOST OF SHERRY BIDDISON makes another lunge toward my girls.

"What is your problem?" I ask tersely.

"You're just like her," the spirit says. "Always back-talking and spouting your opinions. A woman's place is supporting her man, not trying to upstage him."

I'm totally perplexed. "Who are we talking about?"

"Virgilian."

"Your daughter-in-law?"

"You're a smart one, girlie," Sherry says.

I relay all of this information to my team. Although they're at a safer distance than I am, they're following along with their meters, recorders, and camera equipment.

Celia's face glows in the light of her laptop screen. "The barometric pressure dropped severely just now and there have been two cold spots recorded as well."

"What does all of this mean?" I hear Donn ask.

"We've got a shitload of paranormal activity going on," Becca says. Then she catches herself. "Oops, sorry, Mayor. I meant—"

Mayor Shy snickers. "I think *shitload* is an accurate description."

I can't be bothered with the scientific report behind me, though. Sherry Biddison's energy is off the charts, my central nervous system is on high alert, and I'm definitely connected to this woman. A melancholy washes over me as I sense her pain and feel the suffering she experienced when she—

OMG!

Bones breaking. Organs battered. Spinal injury. Blood . . . blood . . . blood . . .

"Oh, Sherry," I say sadly. "You fell down the stairs, cracked your skull, broke your back, and then bled to death. That's how you died."

The woman lunges at me again. "*She* was supposed to go down the stairs!"

My left shoulder aches, and unexpectedly my back feels as if several vertebrae are cracked. I'm empathizing with what the spirit suffered when she plunged down the stairs. Hitched breathing clogs in my throat, and I struggle to suck in a solid gust of much-needed air.

"Kendall, are you okay?" Celia asks from over my shoulder.

I can't respond. The images that Sherry is feeding to me are so vivid. So hurtful. So intentional.

"You . . . you tried to kill Virgilian? Your own daughter-in-law?" I double over and grab hold of my belly. "And she was pregnant. Oh my God. What kind of horrid person were you,

Sherry Biddison? You purposely plotted to kill the woman who was carrying your grandchild!"

Bile rises in my throat; the burning sensation eats away at my esophagus. How could anyone be so cruel? I envision Virgilian Biddison, seven months pregnant, fighting off her mother-in-law as she attempted to toss her down the stairs. But Virgilian was strong and she did everything she could to protect her baby from the vicious attack.

"You're a horrible person!" I eke out. "I don't want to help you pass into the light. You deserve to burn in hell!"

Father Mass screams out at me, "Kendall! What are you saying?"

I twist around with tears stinging my eyes. "She tried to kill her daughter-in-law and her grandchild!"

Father Mass crosses himself. "Lord have mercy on her soul."

"You ain't kidding!" I shout.

Suddenly, I think of poor Emily trapped in the burning car, struggling to get out and doing all she can for her unborn child. A child who might not have lived after all that. Or, a child who might be out there with no clue of who its mother is or what happened to her. At least Virgilian Biddison fought off Sherry, so the joke was on her.

Sherry shows her teeth to me like a she-wolf in the wild. "That Yankee had no business joining my family and ruining our good name. I didn't want that child. I didn't want her in our lives. She deserved to die!"

All the emotions I'm feeling jam up like rubberneckers on an interstate highway, and I lose my shit. "Virgilian didn't deserve to die, Sherry. You did!"

With that, the spirit whirls around me like a tornado, filling the air with her abhorrence of not only her own family but also—me. I'm stricken with a sense of vertigo; I feel myself falling out of control, tumbling, in fact, head over heels. Holy crap! I'm spiraling down the stairs as shouts of *Kendall* sound out, like I can do anything about it. My right hip hits the banister, my left knee the stair. My head cracks against the wall. Arm into the railing. Head—*bam!* Other knee—*crack!* Someone help me! Stop this!

Thhhhwappp!

I land—frickin' hard—at the bottom of the staircase. I'm totally going to have one amazingly humongoid bruise, if not some broken bones. Son of a bitch! Sherry pushed me. She. Pushed. Me. That bitch.

As battered as I am, I feel no pain.

Warmth.

Comfort.

Wetness?

"Kendall! Oh my God! Holy shit! Kendall! Talk to me!"

Who's saying that? I can't tell if it's Loreen, Becca, Celia, Taylor, Donn, or Shelby-Nichole. All of the voices blend together in a dissonance of tones. Faces spin around my head as hands reach out to me, moving me, touching me, feeling my arms and legs.

Yet nothing.

Their touch is invisible. Ineffective.

I can't move. No matter how hard I try. Nothing's working.

Jesus! Please don't let this be my vision coming true.

I try to move my eyes, but they seem heavy and sticky. Are my eyelids even open? No, they're not. However, I still see what's going on.

Taylor . . . don't cry.

Oh crap . . . even Celia's crying. And Becca too.

"Call nine one one!" Father Mass shouts at the top of his lungs.

Donn responds. "I've called my security!"

Loreen grasps my hand. I can't feel it. Numbness skitters through me. "Kendall, please talk to me . . . please . . . can you hear me? Squeeze my hand."

Before I know it—hours, minutes, seconds, nanoseconds later—I seem to be floating above everyone else. The view of the house changes, and I see the wall portraits in closer detail. Dirt covers the tops of the frames, years of thickness. Oops— guess the maids don't clean there. I'll have to remember that little detail.

Am I flying? I'm at least floating.

Holy Mother of God . . . I'm floating.

Then it hits me like a wet noodle across the cheek.

"I'm having an out-of-body experience!" I say to no one.

Sure, I'm an investigator. I've read about OBEs. Celia's talked about how awesome it would be to have one and I've always pooh-poohed her. And here I am, actually having one.

Okay. I need to remain calm. I need to think.

Celia, the science geek, had prattled on to me about a month ago about this book called *Journeys Out of the Body,* by Robert Monroe. He's apparently some old dude who made up this stuff forever ago, in the 1960s. Yet Celia treats his book like it's her paranormal bible. I tap into the corner of my brain that's slightly photographic in memory and try to think hard on Celia's obsession about this book. Oh yeah ... I'm remembering this: there's something about the astral body or state of being out of the body that is affected by gravity. If I can relax and go completely limp, I'll drift back down to the floor like a feather or a bubble.

As I'm even thinking this, I feel myself descending and gingerly touching down on the carpeted hallway. My fingers thread into the fine hand-sewn Chinese rug, and I can sense every fiber passing through my palms as if I'm pushing through a bed of a thousand needles, yet there's no pain. There's just this weird tingly sensation.

Okay. . . . that's sort of cool.

Next, I push all of my weight downward until I press into a solid surface. Jiminy Christmas! Are those the floorboards underneath? At first I'm totally wigged until I remember Celia preaching on about that Monroe guy's talking about penetrating surfaces depending on their density. Whoa—this is too much for my nonscientific mind to comprehend. So much information and knowledge seems to automatically be there for me. Does this mean Celia's part of my brain? Or I absorbed all of her chitter-chatter by some sort of osmosis?

So, yeah . . . the wood floor, more dense, more difficult to penetrate. Makes sense. With a firm nudge of my hands—at least, I think these are still my hands—I begin passing through the floor as well. Are my arms really dangling all the way through? I mean, if someone went down to Shelby-Nichole's basement and looked, would my arms be hanging out of the ceiling?

Holy Freakasaurus! This is too much. I jerk back up, and I'm floating in the center of the room again. Riiiiight—like that's normal.

Normal? What exactly is normal now?

Wait! Celia talked about some silver cordy thing that tethers your soul to your body. If I'm truly having an OBE, that cord has to be there, keeping me attached to my physique. I feel around the back of my head. Other than my knotted and twisted hair, there's nothing there. No string, no thread, no cord. Frantic, I shove my hands into my curls, tugging and searching for a sign that I'm still one with my body.

All right. Enough of this bullshit. An OBE was fun for a moment. Not enjoying it anymore. Ready to go home. I want my bed. I want Sonoma the bear. I want my mom. Damnit, I want my body.

Okay. One, two, three. *Snap.*

That didn't work.

David Blaine I'm not. I'm not even close to being David Copperfield, or any other David.

I need some magic now!

Here we go. Annnnnnnnd . . . jump.

The sounds of Taylor screaming bloody murder make me glance down at the T-shirted and jeaned figure lying supine on the floor. Loreen is there holding one hand. Celia is cradling the head. And Jason . . . oh, wow—Jason's here!

"Jason!"

He can't hear me, though. My sweet boyfriend, who said he wouldn't come on this investigation. Somehow he's here. Holding . . . *me?* Wait a sec. Crappity-crap! That is, like, *my* freakin' body down there. I'm up here taking a gander at it. How do I get back in there?

"Kendall—I begged you not to do this investigation. Oh, baby. Don't leave me." The plea in Jason's voice makes me want to cry. Yet I have no tears in my eyes. Do I even have eyes? I attempt to rub my face, but nothing happens.

The mayor's special security force bursts in with a medical supply kit. An oxygen mask is placed over my nose and mouth. Like that's going to do any good. I'm at death's door! Why can't anyone hear me?

Oh my frickin' God! It's happened. Sherry Biddison has made my vision come true. She has taken me to the brink of death.

You bitch!

I hear her sinister laugh. *Now you know how I feel.*

The ambulance arrives. I sit in a corner near the ceiling watching as the EMTs strap a blood pressure cuff on me and begin taking my vitals. None of this matters. I'm bleeding internally. My spleen is ruptured. One of my lungs is in the process of collapsing.

"Yes, this is Mayor Shy. Tell David and Sarah Moorehead to meet us at the hospital immediately. There's been a terrible accident."

I see Donn make the call, but I don't know who it's to. The details of the room are fading . . . fading . . . and I can't hold on. Oh, where is that stupid cord that's supposed to be attached to me? Was it severed when I took the header down the stairs?

A wall of blond hair sweeps into view. "This is all my fault," Donn says through tears. "I never should have allowed this."

Loreen is comforting her. Massimo is comforting Loreen. Celia and Becca hold hands. Taylor grips her brother.

And I'm floating free . . . free of this . . .

There's nothing I can do to stop it. The warmth embracing me permeates me with love and joy and happiness and peace and other words I fail to find right now. I start up this long, flowing staircase—oh no, not another one!—into a white light. Its glow beckons to me like nothing I've ever seen. I hear the sweet melody of a piano accompanied by a string quartet.

I cross a small wooden bridge over a rainbow stream. A lush

garden with full blooms of every flower imaginable—roses, hydrangeas, baby's breath, and orchids—dancing in the sunlight cascading through the fluffy clouds.

A familiar *meow* catches my ear and I turn to face the sound.

From the bank of the stream, a flash of black and white comes at me, furry tail up straight in the air. *Meow!* he says again.

"Smokey? Is that you?"

He breaks into a run and bounds up to me, rubbing against my leg with his cheek, neck, and tail.

How can this be? This is my kitty Smokey. The one who was accidentally run over by the FedEx truck years ago. Yet he's . . . here? Where *is* here? Is this the famed rainbow bridge I've read about so many times? Where your beloved pet greets you before you both cross over into . . .

No.

No.

No way.

A white lattice gazebo sits at the far end of the garden, a fountain of crystal blue water on the side of it. I see the back of a woman sitting in a rocking chair, the soft breeze ruffling her gray curls. Cautiously, I approach, trying not to disturb her.

But she calls out, "Come now, Smokey."

He begins to purr and runs up ahead of me, leading me down the path to the gazebo and the woman. I automatically follow, no questions asked. My feet aren't even touching the ground in this weird float-trot I've got going on.

I approach the three stairs, and I'm suddenly reaching my hand out to the older woman.

"May I join you, ma'am?"

Her charming beauty astounds me. Perfectly preserved and ageless. Yet exactly the woman I remember she was in her late sixties.

"Of course you can, my darling Kendall. I've been expecting you."

I swallow hard. My heart seems like it will burst with all the love filling it.

"Gr-Gr-Grandma Ethel!"

And I fall into her open arms.

Chapter Fourteen

It's the best hug I've ever had in my life.

I push back slightly and smile into my grandmother's face.

"They told me you were coming, child, and I didn't believe them." She takes a lace handkerchief and dabs at my eyes. "It's way too soon for you to be here."

My head swivels as I take in the awe-inspiring scenery, which seems to sparkle as if it's just been buffed by an army of maids and a case of Mr. Clean.

"Where exactly is here?" I ask, biting my bottom lip.

She waves the handkerchief around in the air. "Oh, you know . . ."

No, I don't, exactly—that's why I asked. I hold my tongue, though. I've never felt so warm and loved and comforted and supported. It's like I don't have a care in the world as I sit in a chair next to my grandmother in this lovely locale.

I swallow hard and shift my eyes to hers. "I've missed you so much."

Grandma Ethel rocks in her chair as she folds the hankie and returns it to the pocket of her dress. "I've been watching you, my darling. You and Kaitlin are growing up so fast. You mustn't fight with each other so much. Sisters should be best friends, like Pansy and I were."

Aunt Pansy was Grandma's older sister; she lived in Boca Raton and had nine cats. For Christmas each year she used to send us logs of cheese and pepperoni from Swiss Colony's mail-order. Why I'm thinking about this right now, I have no earthly clue.

Then again . . . is this still Earth?

I take my grandma's hand. "Seriously. Where am I? Am I . . . dead?"

She sets her hand on my cheek and smiles at me. "My darling. You're in some sort of in-between stage. You took a terrible spill down there and your body needs time to heal. While those doctors work on you, it seems your soul wanted to take a little field trip."

"So I'm not exactly alive but I'm not dead . . . yet."

"Semantics," she says with a laugh.

I'm distracted by the purring at my feet. Smokey threads in and out of my legs while he vibrates like a motorboat. I bend down and scoop him into my lap, nuzzling his warm, soft fur. "Baby kitty, I've missed you so much. Why did you run out of the house and in front of that truck?"

"He knew you were coming," Grandma says. "Keeps me company a lot. Never seen him this happy."

"Grandma, forgive me for saying this, but you're, like, dead . . . and so is Smokey. If I'm still alive, how can I see you?"

She lets out a sigh as if searching for the right words. "You see a lot of things, Kendall. It's a skill and a talent that our Lord blessed you with."

I rub Smokey between the ears, and it hits me. "I thought I was just having an out-of-body experience. It's more than that. This is a near-death experience. I've read about it. The white light. The music. The sense of utter happiness." I gaze into Smokey's green eyes. "Seeing your lost loved ones."

"Yes, dear," Grandma confirms. "You're in your own version of paradise until you make your decision."

I scrunch up my mouth and lower my brows. "And what decision is that?"

Grandma says, "To cross over or return to your life."

The thump in my chest lets me know my heart is still beating. I still have life in me.

"You said it's not my time."

"I don't think so," she says.

I gather Smokey tighter into my arms and continue to pet him. He closes his little kitty eyes and curls up. He always was a little snuggle bug. I sit quietly with Grandma Ethel, unsure of how much time passes. The air is so crisp and fresh, no smog or pollution, and no dust from peanut or soybean crops. For a while, we just . . . are.

Grandma breaks the silence. "Your move from Chicago to Radisson hasn't been easy on you."

I shake my head and watch my hair move back and forth. Smokey lifts a paw and swats at a long curl on my chest. "No, ma'am. It's hard being a fish out of water like that. I kind of stick out like a sore thumb. But I've made some really great friends, and I have a nice boyfriend."

Well, I *had* a nice boyfriend.

"People will come and go throughout your life, my child. The ones who really matter will stick to you like peanut butter on the roof of your mouth," my grandma says.

I snicker at her colloquialism.

"That Jason is a sweet boy."

"How? What?" Oh, right—she's been "checking in" on me. Wonder if that means she's seen us make out as many times as Emily has. A hot blush covers me from head to toe just thinking about it.

"Don't you worry your pretty little head any. He's your first love. First loves are always important. I remember my first love. Name was Homer. He was the minister's son. Used to bring me hard candy all the time."

I'm desperately fighting the image of Homer Simpson dating a teenage version of my grandmother. LOL!

"Jason's moving to Alaska," I say somberly. "I guess that means we have to break up. In fact, I think we already sort of have, since we had this big fight."

She reaches over and puts her hand on my arm. "Kendall, your first love will always be with you. Sometimes, though, first loves are simply that. They're the ones you cut your teeth on, so to speak. They're the ones that help you mature and grow and prepare for your more adult relationships."

"Yeah . . . maybe," I say.

"Listen to your grandma. You're young and you have the rest of your life ahead of you—if you so choose. You have to be strong and confident. When you go back, everything is going to be different."

"I know. Jason and Taylor will be leaving soon."

Her eyes soften. "I'm not just talking about that, darling."

Cocking my head the side, I ask, "What do you mean?"

"You're a sensitive girl, and because of that, you'll have challenges in your life. You just need to pay attention to the signs around you that can easily answer the questions you have."

"What questions?" I ask with a question. Okay, she's starting to speak in riddles.

"You'll see, Kendall. You've been blessed with a gift. One inherited through your family. Use your skills wisely as you age. Cleave to those you trust and love. Never doubt yourself."

Smokey stretches and hops out of my lap. Grandma bends to pick him up. "Time for you and me to get going, kitty cat."

I reach out for them. "But wait! There's so much more I want to talk to you about."

She blows me a kiss. "There will be another opportunity. People are worried about you, Kendall. Don't keep them waiting any longer."

"Grandma! Smokey! Don't leave!"

Everything darkens. There's no sound. No light.

I don't know if she is taken from me or I'm taken from her. But immediately, I'm whisked out of the serene garden and dropped unceremoniously into the corner of an antiseptic hospital room, where I see Mom, Dad, and Kaitlin keeping watch over me.

"Guys! Over here!" I shout at them, but they hear nothing.

To my left is . . . well . . . me.

Holy crap! That's me. My physical body is lying supine under the tight white sheets. IVs are hooked into my arm.

My head is bandaged and my brown hair is pulled back from my face. A thick ace bandage encases my right arm. Heart monitors steadily beep away, getting information from the wires attached to my back and chest. A nurse enters to check my vitals and make notes in a chart. Mom looks beat, like she hasn't slept in days. Kaitlin seems bored as she plays with her Nintendo DSi; however, deep down she's scared shitless that her big sister is going to be taken away from her. Dad's hair is unkempt from combing it with his fingers in the time since my accident.

Accident.

The accident.

It was no accident.

I remember clearly everything that happened. Sherry Biddison attacked me, and I took a nasty-ass fall down the stairs at Mayor Shy's house.

Dr. Murphy, my mom's boss, enters the room, trying to be cheerful. "How's my favorite family today?"

Mom lifts sad eyes to the doctor. "Still keeping watch over our girl. It's been three days now and still no change."

He flips through the chart that the ICU nurse hands him. "Her vital signs are strong and her blood pressure is steady. She's recovering nicely from the simple pneumothorax she was suffering from when the ambulance brought her in."

Pnuemo-*what?* Where's Wikipedia when I need it?

Fortunately, my kid sister pipes up. "What does that mean?"

Mom touches her with her hand. "Kendall had a partially collapsed lung from the spill she took down the stairs. The doctors had to put a tube in her chest to gently suction out the air surrounding her lung so her lung could properly expand again."

Kaitlin grimaces. "Like, eww—sorry I asked."

Always the brat.

Dr. Murphy's eyes zip over my chart and he draws a quick breath of air. He then closes my chart and folds it under his arm. He removes his glasses and places them into the front pocket of his white coat. He's not part of the team of doctors that have been attending to me here at Radisson Memorial Hospital. However, owing to his closeness with my mom, he's trying to comfort my family.

"Sarah and David—do you mind if I speak with you two alone?"

Dad turns to my sister and says, "Kaitlin, why don't you run down to the cafeteria and order a milk shake."

She closes the cover of her DSi, rolls her eyes, and tromps out of the room. The nurse follows after her.

Dr. Murphy slides the door closed and then takes a chair next to my mother. "Sarah, you're a nurse, so I'm going to tell this to you straight."

"Of course, Doctor."

Dad moves closer and laces his fingers through Mom's. I slip from the corner of the room over to where my body rests. How can I get back into it? Do I lie down on the bed and hope my spirit melds into my flesh? Do I need Loreen to come tether me to my skin?

I snap my fingers—or at least I think I do. Not really sure it if works in this spirit form I'm in. In any case, I have an idea. I'll go talk to Celia. G'friend has been wanting a paranormal experience, and, boy, do I have one for her.

I stop in my tracks, though, when something Dr. Murphy says knocks me back to semireality.

"—and it seems she's going to need a further blood transfusion."

Dad speaks. "Sarah and I both gave when Kendall came in the other day. The ER nurse said it was standard for family members to donate."

Dr. Murphy sits forward. "I understand that, David. Kendall continues to have internal bleeding, even after we removed her spleen—"

Removed my what? Youch! Great, I'll be scarred for life.

Continuing, he says, "This is more serious, though. She has already received the supply of O negative that Radisson

Memorial had in its bank. We can get some Medevaced out from Atlanta, I was asked to discuss this with you first because of the circumstances."

Mom and Dad exchange knowing glances. "As I'm sure you both know, Kendall is O negative, which means she can be a universal donor. However, she can't receive anything *but* O negative. And both you and your wife are AB positive. So is your youngest, Kaitlin."

"We can explain, Dr. Murphy."

I walk over to my mother and attempt to put my hand on her shoulder to connect with her. I'm not the science geek that Celia is, but I'm smart enough to know that something's not adding up here. "Yeah, Mom, please explain."

How can my own family—my own flesh and blood—*not* be a match for me in terms of a blood donation? That makes no sense. Not Mom? Not Dad? Hell, I'd even take bratty Kaitlin's blood, but hers doesn't match either!

Mom's eyes fill with tears that wet the tips of her dark lashes as she blinks hard.

"There's a reason for that," Mom starts. Her hand goes to her throat as her voice catches. Dad squeezes her shoulder for support. "Kendall isn't our natural-born child. We adopted her at birth."

Chapter Fifteen

Hold the freakin' phone!

Are you kidding me?

I'm . . . *adopted?*

Trembling knees refuse to hold up even my ethereal body, and I collapse to the floor in a heap. WTF? My life so far has been one big farce. Lies. Lies on top of lies. A charade. A sham, travesty, mockery—and an absolutely *ridonkulous* situation.

The rest of my parents' conversation with Dr. Murphy is lost in my tumbled thoughts. My eyes dart between Mom and Dad. Between David and Sarah Moorehead. Who are these people? Where did they get me from? Did I come from the stork? Or from an underprivileged orphanage? Was I a prom baby no one wanted? Was I rescued from a dumpster or dropped off at a baby Safe Haven?

If I had a pulse, I'm sure it would be racing wildly. If I had a heart, I'm sure it would be breaking in half. Let's see the doctors try and mend that.

Everything I've known for seventeen years no longer exists.

I remember back to one of the first times I hung out with Loreen. She hugged me and had some sort of vision that I had lost my mother like she had. Well, damn it all if she wasn't right. Sarah Moorehead, the woman who taught me to tie my shoes and make cookies. The lady who punished me when I was bad and brought me Tylenol for Children when I was sick. The person who took me to my first dance recital and sat in the front row cheering even though I made an ass of myself as one of the mice in *The Nutcracker*. *That* woman is *not* my mother. Loreen once told me that *my* mother died in childbirth. And it's true.

I sit alone in the cold ICU room with my unconscious body. A frame that's bruised and battered and bleeding internally. One in need of further blood transfusions that the people who have clothed, fed, educated, and housed me my whole life can't give me.

Then I realize I'm not alone.

Emily is here.

She wears a hospital gown, not unlike the one my earthly body is wearing. Mine is covered in mauve and teal flowers. Hers is light blue.

There's something different about her this time. She doesn't seem so much like a ghost right now; rather, she looks like a real person. I lift my chin in her direction and link eyes with her. Soft hazel eyes, much like my own. Her hair cascades over her shoulders in loose waves. Sort of like mine—on a good hair day. Emily stretches her hand out toward me and brushes her fingers against my cheek. Her touch is warm and gentle. Warm? How can a ghost be warm?

"Oh, Kendall," she says, her voice not inside my head this time. Her words are clear and distinct, as real as she is right now.

"Emily." I'm barely able to get the word out for fear of acknowledging the truth in my head. "How can I feel you?"

"Because we're on the same plane."

"But I'm not dead . . . yet."

Her eyes widen. "It's not your time, Kendall. It's not."

"That's what Grandma Ethel said." At least she *had* been my grandma; I realize now it was in name only.

I want to cry. No tears form or drop, though. I stare at the woman before me and take in her appearance as I've never been able to do before. Ivory skin untouched by the sun. Delicate hands and small wrists. Eyes so kind and caring. Then again, she has been with me my whole life. All at once, it becomes crystal clear. The lullabies that were hummed to me as a baby. The protection and guidance I've gotten since my awakening. The warnings over visions, dreams, and interactions with spirits who have an ax to grind.

Emily and I just stare at each other.

There are no words exchanged between us.

Hell, I'm psychic, remember? I just . . . know.

"You're my birth mother," I whisper.

She smiles at me and stretches out her arms.

For a moment, I'm at peace. Like when I was in the near-heavenly garden with Grandma Ethel and Smokey. For a second, there's finally an explanation for who I am and where I came from and why I have these abilities. They were inherited. From my family. A family I never knew because of a tragic accident.

Emily cradles me to her, her long-lost love pouring out to me in waves that need no thoughts or words combined with them. Her lips touch my forehead and she rocks me tenderly.

"Everything will be okay."

"But I have so many questions—"

"Shhhh . . . not now. Another day."

"You promise we can talk? You'll quit playing games and tell me everything?"

Emily nods her head. "It's time for you to go back. You have unfinished business."

"But Em—"

She fades away. I hunch over in near exhaustion from the news and events. I'm so tired. I want to sleep. I want to go back to that meadow and play with Smokey. I want to talk to my mom . . . and my . . . mom. So many questions. Not enough answers. I'm dizzy. I'm nauseated. I feel like I've been beaten to within an inch of my life. I need blood. The doctor said so. None in their donor bank. I'm fading fast. No energy to stay in this form.

Rest first.

Tired.

Can't . . .

I trip over to where my body lies in the hospital bed. If I can reconnect even for a little bit, maybe I can make it back. For some ludicrous reason, like useless trivia one needs only to win a game of *Jeopardy!*, I remember another person who is O negative. All I have to do is get a message to them. They can save me.

Then I can save myself.

I'm not quite sure how cool it is to sneak into someone's room like this. Of course, I've been bothered plenty of times by spirits who talk to me throughout the night, keeping me awake with their problems to the point that I practically fall asleep in class. I have no idea of what day it is or what time it is. I just know that it's dark and late.

I can't really explain how I got into the house, but here I am. I don't need to walk up the stairs 'cause I've still got this whole floaty thing going on. At the top of the stairs, I head straight for the room that I've hung out in countless times.

Celia is sprawled out on her queen-size bed. Her black hair is a messy mop. Her tank top is bunched up around her waist, and she has one leg thrown over the covers. She's snoring like . . . a man.

Not sure how I can wake her up. I can't touch her and I can't move items in her room to get her attention.

Out of the blue, I get the sense that I'm being watched. Not by Celia.

"Seamus!" I say.

Woof!

Celia's English bulldog licks at me; his tongue connects with nothing but air.

"Seamus, you can see me, buddy."

Woof . . . booooowwww . . . woof, woof!

The noise from the dog rouses Celia and she groans.

This is working! I keep waving my hands at Seamus, riling him up. He barks heartily, digging his paws into the carpet like he always does when I start to play with him.

"Shuuuuuuddddup . . ." comes from underneath the pillow.

"We're getting to her, boy," I say.

Seamus continues. I hop up on the bed next to Celia and pat next to me. The hefty bulldog does everything in his power to follow me. This causes Celia to bolt up in the bed and flip over.

"Dog, you have *gotta* be kidding me." She rubs the sleep out of her eyes with her fists. "What is your major malfunction?"

My partner in crime paws at me right on cue. "Come on, boy. Show her I'm here."

Now fully awake, Celia flicks on the light next to her bed. I can see her immediately switch into full ghost-huntress mode. She watches Seamus carefully as he tries to play with me. I hold my hand up high and snap, getting him to balance on his hind legs. Celia's eyes follow his movement as she examines the spectacle before her.

She crawls out of bed and nabs her EMF detector and a digital recorder. Good girl.

I dash a quick prayer upward. "God, I hope this works."

Hundreds of times, I've been in the position to listen to a spirit without the help of modern technology. However, Celia's not blessed with the psychic abilities that I have. Instead, my best friend is gifted with an open mind, a sense of adventure, and an overwhelming belief that she *will* have her own genuine, bona fide paranormal experience. Who'da thunk it would be me giving it to her?

She flips on the EMF detector and begins a scan of her room, following Seamus around. "What are you seeing, Seamus? Is there a ghost here? Come on . . ."

I place myself directly in front of the meter, hoping I can make something—anything—register. Since I'm not officially dead, merely in this in-between stage, I don't know if I have the full energy to make anything register. Certainly I have the ability to leave her an EVP, though.

"Ceeeeeeeeeeeeelia!" I scream at the top of my lungs.

Seamus echoes my call with a howl of his own.

She glimpses around her dark room. "Someone is here, aren't they?" The red light indicator on her digital recorder clicks on. "Hi there," she says. "My name is Celia Nichols and I'm well versed in attempted communication with the spirits.

I have a device here in my hand that can record your voice if you're willing to speak into it." She adjusts closer to where Seamus is nipping at my feet. "Just talk into the red light and I will be able to listen to whatever message you have for me."

Well, this is certainly interesting. I've been on the other end of the recorder many times. Never thought I'd be trying this so soon. Celia and I have even been laughing and kidding around about contact from the other side recently. I sincerely hope that I can get through to her.

I sit on the floor directly in front of Celia. Her silver recorder is perched between us.

"What is your name?" she asks.

"Kendall Moorehead, you dodo bird."

"What time period are you from? Are you a survivor of the Civil War?"

I roll my eyes. "Good Lord, no! Celia, it's me! Can you hear me?"

This goes on for quite some time, with Celia questioning me like I'm some random spirit. I don't know how to get across to her that it's me. There's no spiritual-contact code or secret phrase we planned so each of us will know who the other one is.

"I know!"

I bend down and put my mouth as close to the recorder as possible. I speak the only language the two of us share perfectly. Something we connected on the first time we met. Mentally,

I scan my catalog of quotes from the Bard. I'm sure *he* will be able to get my message across.

Weariness encompasses me. I'm running out of strength.

So tired.

To sleep.

Perchance to dream.

Or in my case . . . just to wake up to my normal life.

I'm ready to go back.

Chapter Sixteen

Beep. Beep. Beep. Beep. Beep.

What *is* that annoying sound?

Beep. Beep. Beep. Beep. Beep.

My nose itches. I reach to scratch it and—

Why are there tubes and wires connected to me?

Beep. Beep. Beep. Beep. Beep.

Stop that!

I open my eyes and blink into the fluorescent light overhead. Man, that's bright.

I try to swallow, but my throat is dry as a bone.

Grogginess envelops me in a haze of confusion. Where am I? What's with the beige ceiling tiles overhead? Why does my back hurt? Man, I totally have to pee. Everything inside me says it wants to get up and go to the bathroom, yet nothing reacts. I seem pinned down to the bed. Not even my bed. Where are my pillows? This isn't my Synchilla blanket. And where is Sonoma the bear?

I lift my hand again to swat at the itch now tiptoeing across my cheek. A clear tube hangs down, filled with a liquid that's slipping into my skin. An attempt to stretch only brings massive tingles and damn-near fiery jolts through me. I truly feel like I've been beaten within an inch of my life. It nearly takes an act of Congress, but I manage to twist my head to the right. My mom is asleep in a chair with her King James Bible clutched to her bosom. I hear the television overhead sounding softly.

"The Bruins beat the Islanders six to four today—" *Click.* "—the President called today for sanctions against—" *Click.* "—buy one Shamwow and get another free—" *Click.* "—I'll take Potent Potables for eight hundred, Alex—" *Click.*

"Goooooooood grief," I say in a moan, mustering up all the strength I have. "Pick a channel already, would ya?"

Jason drops the remote and is instantaneously by my side. "Kendall! Kendall! You're awake!"

"Of course I am." I try to roll to my side with no luck. "Who can sleep with the mondo channel-surfing going on?"

He laughs until he begins to choke up. "Miss Sarah—she's awake!"

Mom rouses in the chair next to me, then drops her Bible to the cushion. She pushes past Jason and flings herself over me. "Oh, my baby. My baby! Kendall, are you okay? Talk to me!"

I attempt to lift my right arm to hug her back; however, it's encased in a rather large bandage. "From the looks of it, I'd say—no?" My weak attempt at humor is lost on the visitors in my room. Mom begins crying and I can see the intense emotions in Jason's face too as he shifts his jaw from side to side.

In the crease of his elbow, I make out a bulky Band-Aid. He follows the path of my eyes and smiles at me.

Then it all comes whooshing back to me, like a tsunami wave.

Everything.

The investigation at Mayor Shy's house.

The altercation with Sherry Biddison.

The ascension of some sort to a realm where Grandma Ethel and Smokey greeted me.

The sensation of utter peace and bliss.

And then, the coming back to ... the discovery.

Jason takes my hand. "You've been bad off, K. So I donated some blood to help out," he says proudly.

I blink hard again. "I know."

I stare past him to my mom—who ... isn't my mom at all. Yet she is. My heart aches as I witness tears of relief gushing down her weary face. Somehow I know she hasn't had a moment's rest since I tumbled down that staircase like Scarlett in *Gone With the Wind*. Mom takes my hand from Jason and she kisses the top before placing it against her cheek. I don't pull away or anything. Why would I?

We stay this way for a few moments. I close my eyes and relish the love being sent to me in such a simple act of affection.

"There's my girl!" Dad says, bursting into the room. "If you wanted attention, Kendall, you could have just said something," Dad teases, with a wink of his eye.

"Hi, Dad," I eke out. Dad. Only not.

With both parents here now, one on either side of me, I have to speak up.

I alternate my gaze between the two of them. "I know."

"Know what, baby?" Mom asks.

My chest constricts in an ache I've never experienced as I attempt to shuttle the words out of me for all to hear. "I . . . I know I'm adopted."

Mom's face falls. "Oh."

"And I know that my spirit guide, Emily—the one who was my imaginary friend so many years ago, the woman who Celia sketched and showed to you both—*she* is my real mother."

Dad seems stricken by this. He turns to my mother. "Sarah? Did you—"

Hand on her heart, she swears, "No, never."

Jason—just as shocked by this revelation—exits the hospital room quietly, pulling the door closed behind him. Now it's just me and Mom and Dad. Me and the Mooreheads. The people who raised me as their own.

"Please tell me," I beg.

Mom wipes away more tears. "Oh, Kendall. Now's not the time to get—"

"Really, Mom. I need to hear this."

With a deep exhalation, Sarah Moorehead begins the tale. "All I know is that I was on duty in the neonatal ICU the night of December twenty-second. I was called down to the ER to assist because they'd just brought in a young woman who'd been in a horrid car accident out on the interstate, and she was going into labor." Mom stops a minute to compose herself as she remembers the night that changed so many lives.

"I never knew the girl's name," Mom says, her eyes misty with memories. "She was in such a bad way. Only seven months along in her gestation."

I try not to consider that *I* was said "gestation."

She continues. "The girl and her friend were hit head-on by a drunk driver, and their car caught fire. The paramedics weren't able to save the driver. So sad, really. No wallet with an ID, and the poor thing's body was so charred, they weren't even able to identify the person through dental records. But the woman was removed from the car with the Jaws of Life."

Of course she was, I think. I envisioned all of that in my dream. My dream of Emily's past.

"While the doctors worked on saving the woman's life, I assisted with your birth. It was an easy one, I must say. You were a squirmy little thing, fighting your way into this world." Her eyes get glassy. "When the doctor handed you to me to clean you off, you wrapped your tiny little hand around my pinkie and held on tight."

I adjust my hand in exactly the same manner as Mom tells more of the story.

"I knew the poor woman wasn't going to make it. She hadn't been wearing her seat belt and was thrown into the dashboard. There was massive trauma to her head and chest. The impact itself is what caused her premature labor and your impulsive birth." She laughs at the thought. "But miracle among miracles, the woman fought to stay conscious through all of it."

"I wanted to see my little girl," Emily says next to me.

"Emily," I say in a whisper. Gazing into Mom's face, I tell her, "Emily's right here with us now."

I can see the disbelief in my mother's eyes at first. Then she glances about, as if she's looking for the young woman she once tried to save.

I prod Mom along. "Emily just told me that she knew she was going to die. She wanted to see me before passing on."

"I understand," Mom says with a sniff. "I did everything I could to assure the girl that her baby would be cared for. That we would give her the best medical attention possible. You see, your father and I had been married for seven years. We'd tried having a baby. I even had a miscarriage after an in vitro procedure. I truly believed that God had special plans for us, something other than us having our own child. So when you were placed in my arms in that emergency room, I felt an immediate bond and connection like I'd never had before with any of the other hundreds of babies I'd worked with."

"And I knew that," Emily says. I repeat everything to my parents as she shares it with me. "Sarah talked to me about wanting a baby of her own and that was why she worked in the neonatal unit. She promised me that my baby would be delivered safely and would have a fighting chance at life. I knew my own life was over. I knew I was alone. I knew no one had a clue where I was, the situation I was in, or even what my name was. I was on my way from Wisconsin to St. Louis when we were in that wreck in Chicago. I was going home for Christmas."

"Who were you with, Emily? Was it my dad?"

She shakes her head. "That doesn't matter right now, Kendall."

Oooh! I hate when she does that to me.

Mom seems to sense my frustration and continues with the story. "The young woman—Emily, you say?—was fading fast. Her vitals were slipping and her heart rate was slowing. I wanted so much for her to hold you in her arms, even if only one time."

I can't help but cry along as my mom tells this. Hot, sticky tears that blend into the bandage on my head and into my hair. I don't care, though. Not right now.

"Emily held you and kissed you. She said, 'Name her Kendall . . . it's a family name.'"

Jerking to attention, I laser-beam my eyes at my ghost. "Your last name is Faulkner. Was that your married name? Maiden name? My dad's name? What? Throw me a bone here."

"In due time, Kendall. Let Sarah tell the story."

"What?" Mom asks.

I smirk. "Just like a mother. She's telling me to be quiet and let you finish."

Mom tries to laugh, only more tears come. She dabs them away with a tissue. "Emily passed you back to me and made me promise to take care of you. She wanted you to be raised in a loving home and for you to never know the tragedy that brought you into this world. Emily died a Jane Doe at Northwestern Hospital and remains that way today. I watched over you in an incubator for three months while you continued developing and growing stronger every day. Your father and I made all the necessary arrangements with the hospital and the local authorities to adopt you. I honored the woman who bore you by naming you Kendall." Mom tightens her grip on me as she weeps harder. "Have no qualms about it, though. *You* are *my* daughter."

My vision is completely watery and wavy, like a funhouse mirror. I sniffle hard before finding the words. "I know, Mommy," I say, reverting to my childhood, almost. "I know I should feel all sorts of negative stuff right now, finding out I'm adopted. But I only feel gratitude to you for letting me be part of your life. For *wanting* me and never letting me feel like I didn't belong to you." I address the spirit next to me. "And you, Emily. Through a nasty car crash and being in the hospital, you only worried about me. It was totally kismet that brought you to that hospital and to my mom. Thank you. Thank you both."

Mom reaches out in faith. "Thank you, Emily. You gave me the greatest gift of all."

I wipe away my own tears and address the two women, one on each side of me. "I've watched enough Lifetime movies to know I should scream bloody murder about lies and cover-ups and not being wanted or what have you. But honestly, I feel only gratitude at this point." I glance at Mom. "You and Dad have been amazing for letting me be part of your lives. And Emily . . . in your final moments, you were only thinking of me—your unborn child. You're both amazing women."

As I peer at the two women who mean so much to me, all I can do is thank them . . . and thank God. It's not every day you get a second chance at life. That's exactly what I've gotten.

"Mmm, lime Jell-O. Can I have it?"

Celia bounds into my hospital room and starts eyeballing my half-eaten lunch. Apparently, I've existed these past days on a diet of glucose and saline. Now I get chicken broth, tea, and gelatin as they build me back up to solid foods. I don't think anyone—even my best friend—is gonna scarf my dessert.

"Paws off," I say kiddingly.

"I give! I give!" Celia throws her hands up in the air to fend me off, and I notice a bandage that matches Jason's on her left arm.

"What happened?"

"This thing? You should know."

"I don't understand."

Celia grins wide at me. "Come off it, Kendall. Last night. My bedroom. The EVP session?"

I so don't know what she's talking about. Do I?

She pulls her Sony recorder from her pants pocket and sets it on my rolling table. "You promised me that you'd help me

have a paranormal experience, and you lived up to it. Well—
not lived, maybe. I'd say you were in some sort of state of unconsciousness somewhere between the world we know here
and the ethereal world where so many of our, er, clients exist."

"What *are* you talking about, Nichols?" I think she's finally
gone off the deep end.

"Hit Play."

With her recorder in my palm, I press the button and start
listening. It's Celia having a very professional conversation
with what she thinks is a spirit inhabiting her bedroom. Her
questions are normal for an EVP session.

"You're doing great," I say. "I especially like it when Seamus
chimes in."

"You seriously don't remember? Keep listening."

What*evah.*

Then I'm startled when I hear a rumbled voice through
the static that sounds surprisingly like me. "It'sssssssssssssssss
Kennnnnnn-dallllll."

"Shut up! That did not just say it was me." I'm too stunned
to laugh.

Then I hear Celia on the recording. "Kendall? Is that really
you?"

"Yessssssssssss."

"Tell me what you need from me," she says on the recording. Then Celia turns to me. "Ready for this? Longest class-A
EVP evah! I had Becca run it through the Audition software
and clean it up. This is what we got."

She presses Play again, and I'm floored by what I hear:

"*'A minist'riiiiing angel shall muh sistah be, / When thou liest hooooooowling.'*"

I sit up in bed, despite the searing pain it causes to my fresh spleen-removal stitches. "Holy shit, Celia! That's *Hamlet,* act five."

"Scene one," she says with a giggle. "First time old Will Shakespeare's been quoted by a spirit and captured on tape, eh?"

I somehow recollect this. "I needed O negative blood and I knew that was your blood type. I reached out to you, Celia!"

She shows me her bandaged arm again. "And I answered the call. As did Jason."

"Both of you?"

"Yup. He's O neg too. Imagine that. Ironically, Taylor's not. Otherwise, you'd be blood brothers with all of us."

Jason did that for me . . . even though we've been on the outs. I'm stricken by a memory of talking to Grandma Ethel about first loves. Jason's just that—a boy who loved me when I needed it the most. And what do you know: he pokes his head in my room right now.

"Hey, you," he says. "Hey, Celia."

"Blood brother. We were just talking about you."

He scratches his head. "Yeah, well, it was the least I could do for you, Kendall. You always said we were connected. Now we really are. Not just by our bracelets."

Mine had been removed by the medical personnel, but it's

back on my wrist. The hematite is warm to my touch, letting me know that Jason and I will be all right.

Celia begins to whistle. "Okay then. My work here is done and I shall be on my way. As you say, Kendall: love ya; mean it!" She bows, waves, and exits stage right.

"Such a drama queen," I say with nothing but love and respect.

Jason eases himself onto the edge of my hospital bed. "Speaking of queens, you know the school's end-of-winter dance is next weekend. I don't know if you'll be up and about, but if you want, we can rent a wheelchair for you."

I beam at him. "Are you asking me to go to the dance with you?"

I can't believe he's actually blushing. "Yeah, of course I am, Kendall."

"Our farewell to each other?" Mom told me that Mr. Tillson delayed their move to Alaska because of my hospitalization.

Jason nods sadly. "I can't help it, K."

I reach out, and we weave the fingers of our braceleted hands together. "I'd be honored to go with you. There's a fabulous dress at the store next to Loreen's that would look great."

He kisses me softly. "You always look great to me. You'll be the most beautiful girl there."

Hearing his words and knowing how lucky I am, I believe I will be.

CHAPTER SEVENTEEN

"WHO'S IDEA WAS THAT Under the Sea Disney theme from the nineties for the dance?" Celia asks as she helps me out of my wheelchair.

"Courtney Langdon," Taylor tells us. "What do you expect?"

"At least she ordered food," I quip, taking a jab at Courtney's well-documented upchucking after meals at school.

"Bad one, Kendall. Baaaad one," Becca says.

Mom greets us in the front foyer with a tray of popcorn and chocolate chip cookies. She's really turned into the quint-essential Southern hostess. "How was the formal?"

It was an evening to remember. Jason and I danced to every slow song they played. Of course, he had to hold me up most of the time because I'm still weak as a newborn kitten. It was so sweet. He let me stand on his feet as he moved us along. Clay and Celia were adorable, discussing some program they saw on the Discovery Channel most of the night. Taylor and Ryan made out when the teachers weren't looking, and Becca and Dragon spiked the punch. Special memories that I will always cherish of a time we'll never recapture, especially since Jason and Taylor will be moving to Alaska soon.

"Awesome," I say, keeping out most of the details of the evening. "Taylor was crowned queen!"

She lifts the rhinestone tiara into the air and waves heartily like Queen Elizabeth II. *"Merci! Merci!"*

"That's fantastic, girls. Make yourselves at home and stay up as late as you'd like."

"Wow, your mom is like a whole new relaxed person," Becca whispers to me.

"I think it was my near-death experience that brought everything to light in our relationship. Not that it wasn't good, but it was strained because of my whole psychic awakening."

There's a tap at the front door. It's after one in the morning. Please don't tell me it's someone searching for ghost hunters. I'm so not ready to go there again.

"It's Jase," Taylor says.

I make my way slowly to the door and see him standing there with his tuxedo tie loose around his collar and the top two buttons undone. He holds up my small black beaded evening bag. "You left this in my Jeep."

"Thanks," I say and then purse my lips at him.

He tugs me out the door onto the porch. "Can we sit in the swing for a minute?"

"Sure."

We park ourselves on the bench and he puts his arm around me. "So I'm leaving soon . . ."

"I know."

He clears his throat. "It'll be hard to date when we're like a kajillion miles from each other."

I fiddle with the elastic on his hematite bracelet. "I know that too."

"I'll always love you, Kendall."

My hand covers his mouth and I stop his next words. "We don't have to do this, Jason. I mean, we're not breaking up because we want to, but because we have to. You'll always be one of my best friends and we can't lose that. There's e-mails and Facebooking and all that."

He smiles bright at me. "You're amazing, you know that? Don't ever change."

I kiss him soundly, enjoying the feel of what may be our last intimate moment. "Yeah, well, you don't change either. I don't want to hear about you doing things in Alaska like shooting wolves from helicopters or anything barbaric like that."

"I promise."

At that moment, his bracelet snaps off in my hand, and the magnetic hematite beads tumble off into his lap.

"Whoa! What just happened?" he asks.

My bracelet breaks too. Matching beads spill onto the wooden porch, falling between the cracks in the hundred-year-old building.

"That's the weirdest thing ever," Jason notes.

"Not really." I explain: "See, Loreen told me that we don't wear hematite, it wears us. We take in its energy for as long as we need it. When it's done with us, well, it . . . breaks."

He screws up his mouth. "You mean to tell me that this bracelet knew we were breaking up so it just, like, self-destructed?"

I shrug. "I don't make the rules of the metaphysical world, I just follow them."

Jason pulls me to him. "You are the cutest thing there is. I'm going to miss the hell out of you."

My face is so close I can feel his breath on me. "You haven't left yet."

Man, I love kissing this boy. It's something I will never forget. Not in five minutes, five years, or five lifetimes. Who knows what our futures will bring? Maybe we'll end up at the same college or backpacking through Europe together. Everything happens for a reason, so at this time, I'll simply enjoy the making-out that's happening.

There's a rustle near the front bushes that makes us jump apart. Eleanor, one of my cats, hops up on the railing and wails at me.

"Oh, get over yourself," I say.

But she's merely telling me I have company.

"Shelby-Nichole, is that you?"

She rustles up in her taffeta dress, holding her high heels in her hand. "Colton took me home after the dance and all hell's broken loose. I'm not going back there."

I call to Taylor, Celia, and Becca to come out and join us. They gather around as Shelby-Nichole details her state of mind. "Something was in my room watching me when I got home. I could feel it. It got all cold in the room and I could see my breath."

"It is late February," Becca says.

"In Georgia," Celia notes. "Keep going."

Shelby-Nichole sits and fans herself with her shoes. "Donn left earlier to go see her friend in Atlanta. She said the activity had increased so much that she doesn't want to stay there anymore. Honestly, she's looking into getting the city to destroy the property altogether to get rid of whatever this Sherry woman is doing."

"You can't do that," Celia pleads. "The spirit is attached to the property, yes, but tearing it down will not ease her pain. She has to be dealt with once and for all. She has to go into the light." Celia directs her stare at me.

"I'm scared shitless of that place. *Helllllo*. She tried to kill me!"

"I can't go back there," Shelby-Nichole says weakly. "It's no way to live."

I sigh hard and lean back into the swing. Yeah, I'm petrified of that place. I'm even more terrified when I think of confronting Sherry Biddison again. But something has to be done. Celia's right—she has to cross over.

I'll be damned, though, if I'm going to be the one to help her do it.

I poke my head into Divining Woman Saturday midmorning to find Loreen working on the store's bookkeeping, which totally amazes me because I've barely ever seen her sell anything. Makes me wonder how she stays afloat.

"Look what the cat dragged in," she says with a laugh. "Aren't you a sight for sore eyes."

"Ahh, queen of the clichés, I see." I walk gingerly into the store, still feeling the physical effects from my fall and recent hospital stay.

"The sayings are cliché for a reason."

Lowering myself to the couch, I snag a pack of Rider-Waite tarot cards from the table nearby and shuffle through them. An old familiar friend, almost. How interesting that the cards have enabled me to decipher details of so many other people's lives yet couldn't help me see the particulars of my own.

Loreen grins at me. A knowing look that only adults can give, one that indicates they were right about everything. No words need to pass between us. We truly are kindred spirits, brought together by life's amazing twists and turns.

"I've been praying hard for you, sweetie. You had me so worried."

"I had a lot of people worried," I say jokingly. Our mailbox has been full of cards with get-well wishes and concern. The house has several new plant additions, thanks to all the ones

I got when I was in the hospital. Even my former nemesis Courtney Langdon sent a bouquet of flowers on behalf of the Radisson High cheerleading squad. Though I'm still a relative newcomer to the town, people reached out in my time of need.

"Massimo has me attending his masses regularly," Loreen adds. "I haven't done that since I was a kid."

"See what love can do?"

Her blush is all the indication I need to know that she has fallen hard for my Episcopal priest. Good thing he's not of the Catholic faith so they can maybe get married one day. My intuition tells me that's where they're headed, but I won't spoil the surprise for her.

She walks across the room, takes the cards I've been fidgeting with, and sits down next to me. "Something's bothering you. Your aura isn't glowing right."

"Geesh, where do I start?" The snarkiness rises from me. "I'm healing from a massive blood transfusion from my best friend and my boyfriend; I had a partially collapsed lung; and, apparently, I no longer have a spleen. I don't even have a freakin' clue what I needed a spleen for in the first place. I just know I've got a scar from losing it—but I'm alive. I'm breathing and walking and doing stuff at school. There's just one thing I *don't* want to do anymore."

Loreen's eyes soften. "I talked to Donn Shy. I know what's been going on at her house. It's gotten bad, Kendall."

Suddenly I'm fascinated with the silver zipper on my

hoodie; I tug it up and pull it back down. I try to block my thoughts from Loreen, but it's impossible.

"Talk to me, Kendall."

I heave a sigh and say, "I don't want to be psychic anymore."

Her hand moves to the back of my neck, where she rubs and sends me Reiki energy. "Oh, honey. I've felt that many times. It's not something we can walk away from."

"I read one time that if you eat a lot of olives, the brine in them will actually block your psychic abilities."

"Pure hogwash," she says. "Yes, you can bury your talent and not use it, just as if you were musically inclined but chose not to practice your instrument anymore. It's a choice only you can make." Loreen strokes my hair. "People like you and me, Kendall. We have something not a lot of other people have. A rare gift that helps, not hurts."

I drop my eyes down. "I got hurt wicked bad."

"Yeah, you did."

My pulse rockets away like it's on some sort of illegal street drug. I'm dizzy and confused and I really just need someone— anyone with more rational thinking than me at the moment— to tell me what's right. I muster up the courage to say "I don't want to ghost hunt anymore."

"Have you told your friends this?"

I shake my head.

Loreen pushes me more. "If it's because of the near-death experience you told me about, you can't let that stop you."

"Ummm—yeah, I can."

"Kendall, look at me." Loreen pauses as I slowly turn my head. "I'll keep repeating this until I'm blue in the face. You. Have. A. Gift. If you want to give up ghost hunting as you've been doing it formally . . . fine, I understand. However, you can't abandon your God-given talent to help others."

"Why not?" I ask in a whimper I barely recognize as my own voice.

"Because, sweetie," she starts, "if you give up, then they win."

I think hard for a moment, letting her words soak in. "Who is they?"

Her lips flatten together. "The bad elements and entities that exist on the other side. The ones that wreak havoc on the living. Those like Sherry Biddison who cause physical pain and suffering not only to you but to people like Donn and Shelby-Nichole. Who will she hurt next?"

My mentor isn't telling me anything I haven't already mulled over in my mind. I think of Grandma Ethel's words to me during my time—if that's what you can call it—with her. She believes in me. My mom and dad believe in me. So does Loreen and Father Massimo and my team. I need to believe in myself.

There will be a moment in the quiet of my room where I will search my soul and let Loreen's advice sink in. No, I don't want *them* to win. This world is for the living, and those at unrest need peace of their own. I've done it before—I suppose I can do it one last time.

"Okay." I let out a long sigh. Loreen already senses what I'm going to say, I can see it in her eyes. "Get Mayor Shy on the phone. Tell her the ghost huntresses are on the case. We'll take care of Sherry Biddison once and for all."

God help me.

CHAPTER EIGHTEEN

WE DON'T USUALLY DO AN INVESTIGATION on a Sunday night, but tomorrow is a holiday and school's closed. Besides, I want to deal with this entity (1) when Taylor is still in town and on the team; (2) when Father Mass can be with us for extra protection and spiritual guidance; and (3) while I've got the guts to go through with it.

I'm sitting at the foot of my bed in the lotus position doing some deep breathing when I hear a tiny knock at my door.

"Come in," I call out, trying not to break the serene moment I've got going.

"Kendall?"

My little sister stands in the doorway, her hazel eyes bright with curiosity. She's sort of kept her distance since I got home from the hospital. She's only thirteen. Who knows what-all her pea-size brain can handle at this point.—I'm so kidding! "Hey, Kaitlin. What up?"

Her high ponytail swings back and forth as she comes toward me. "Nuthin.'"

"You have questions, don't you?"

"Sort of."

I pat the floor next to me. "Plop it down, sis."

"You're not *really* my sister?"

Wowza. The parentals—true to their word—filled her in on everything. "I'm not your *blood* sister, but we're still siblings, all right."

She hangs her head. "Does that mean you're going to go away?"

I try not to laugh at her innocence. Bless her soul. "No, brat. I'm not going anywhere," I say with love in my voice. "You're stuck with me."

Kaitlin smiles a cheesy grin, one I'm sure she didn't plan to make that large or exuberant. "So we'll always be sisters."

"Absomalutely. And maybe when we both grow up more and get out of our terrible teens, we'll even grow close and be the best of friends."

She places her hand in mine. "I'd totally like that, Kendall."

I clutch her tightly and send her all the loving energy I can.

"So, this Emily ghost lady you talk to—she's, like, your actual mother?"

"That would seem to be the case," I state very matter-of-factly. "I wish you could see her. She's pretty and young and loves me so much. Just like our mom."

As the words leave my mouth, Emily materializes in the rocking chair to my left. She waves and blows a kiss at me.

"In fact," I tell Kaitlin, "she's here with us now. Do you want to ask her anything?"

"Umm . . . yeah. Will I be psychic like you one day?" Dare I say I see excitement in my kid sis's eyes?

Emily shrugs. "Psychic ability is usually passed down from blood relatives. Unless Sarah and David have the gift somewhere in their past, it's not likely Kaitlin will. You could guide her, though, Kendall. Teach her what you've learned. Open her mind, if for no other reason than so she'll have a spiritual awakening to the possibilities that lie between heaven and earth."

"Emily says probably not, but if you ever think you're feeling anything or seeing anything, you come to me, okay? I'm still your big sister and I'm here for you, no matter what."

Kaitlin awkwardly leans over and wraps her gangly arms around me. She's still got so much growing up to do. So innocent and so much ahead for her. I'll be here for her. "Love you, Kendall."

"Awww . . . I love you too, Kati-did," I say, using my baby nickname for her.

Just as quickly as she entered my room, she trots out again, like she hasn't a care in the world. The difference four years in age makes.

"Kaitlin's lucky to have you," Emily says.

"I'm lucky to have *you*."

"She needs you in her life. And to know that you'll never abandon her."

"Like you've never abandoned me."

Emily gazes off a bit. "It's true I've been with you, Kendall. Not as a real mother should have, but in the best way possible.

They say souls get tied together when one dies and one is born in the same location. I've stayed with you to watch over you, even when your parents disregarded what you saw as a little girl. I chose to step into the background as you grew up and became the amazing young woman you are today. I had to be here to help you through your awakening. One I never experienced but that my mother and grandmother did."

"What are their names, Emily? How can I find my real family?"

"You're with your real family, Kendall."

"Emily . . ."

She reaches her transparent hand out to me and I almost feel her touch. "You're safe now, Kendall. Everything's going to be okay."

"You're still going to be with me, aren't you?" I say, dread filling my voice. "Now that I've found you, I can't lose you again."

Her smile radiates her love for me. How did I never recognize this before? "I've stayed tied to you for long enough. I wanted you to know the truth, but it was never my place to show it to you. Now that you know, you're stronger for it. It's time that I go."

Tears sting my eyes. "No!"

"Yes, Kendall."

"But . . . but . . . I have so many questions. I want to know my father's name. I want to know where you're from. How I can find my blood relatives. Who am I?"

"You're Kendall Moorehead. Beloved and treasured daughter of two angels, David and Sarah, who have given you a life I never could have."

"Oh, come on! Emily . . . Mom . . ."

She giggles like a girl. "All in due time. Patience, my dear."

Man, I totally hate when grownups tell me that. Like I can't handle the truth. Who are they, Colonel Jessep?

"Why do you have to go?" I ask softly.

"Because for the first time, Kendall . . ." Emily pauses and then stares up at the ceiling. "I see the light. It's vibrant and intoxicating and I want to go into it now. I want to be at peace."

"I want you to too." I know I'm a selfish cow wanting her to stay. "I can't do this without you. I can't ghost hunt and do psychic readings. I certainly can't face Sherry Biddison tonight."

It's almost as if her finger lifts my chin and her face is directly in front of me. Eyes that match my own gaze down at me, warming my insides. "You can do anything, Kendall. Sherry's not as bad as you're giving her credit for. She's misguided and confused. She needs you to lead her into the light, just like you've done for me. Do what God intended for you, my sweet."

With that, her wispy lips graze my forehead in a tingle I sense in my toes. The tears I shed are for our lost relationship, the closeness we could have shared, but mostly out of gratitude for having a guiding spirit with me all these years.

"Always love and appreciate the Mooreheads. I can't tell

you not to search out our family. Please do remember the ones who chose you."

"I promise, Mom."

And just like that, Emily Faulkner, my spirit guide, my first apparition—my birth mother—dissolves away, like so many other ghosts that I have helped. Only this is the most important one ever.

For the moment, the loneliness is palpable. Like a part of me is gone.

"I'll make you proud of me. I'll fight the good fight tonight and cross Sherry Biddison over. I won't let anything stop me."

I love you, Kendall . . . and then she's gone.

Emily is finally at peace.

CHAPTER NINETEEN

"ARE YOU GOING TO BE ABLE TO DO THIS, KENDALL?" Celia asks.

I stare up at the grand staircase in Mayor Shy's mansion. The same steps I tumbled down to my near death thanks to Sherry Biddison. I won't let her hatefulness and resentment stop me this time. I have to get through this for everyone's sake, especially my own.

"I'm on it, Celia."

"Okay. Base camp is set up, Becca's got the recorders in place, Taylor's wired all of the hot spots with the infrared cameras, and we're ready to go."

A mustiness fills the air, tickling my nose with a time long gone by. A time when women didn't have the rights that men did. An era of discord between nations. Brother against brother. Families against families, all for the love of cotton, slaves, and arrogance, as Rhett Butler so aptly put it. How does Sherry Biddison fit into this puzzle? What is keeping her here? I aim to find out so we can end this once and for all. 'Cause, damn it . . . I need a break. I can't keep up this pace. I've got midterms next week. I've got college apps I need to start filling out. And I have a long-lost family I need to begin searching for.

After tonight.

"Is everyone ready?" I ask. We have more people on our hunt tonight. Loreen and Father Massimo are here for protection. Loreen sprayed each of us with her sage and holy water mixture. Father Mass said a prayer and blessed us all with the sign of the cross on each forehead. I've been praying non-stop since I made the executive decision to do this one more time. God is with me . . . and Emily's strength flows through my veins.

Shelby-Nichole sits back, taking it all in but afraid to get more involved after what happened last time. Her boyfriend—well, *I* think they're now boyfriend and girlfriend—Colton stays by her side. Intuition tells me that he totally digs her and thinks she's the coolest person ever. He doesn't want anything to jeopardize her well-being. Sort of like my Jason, who, despite having to hop a flight westward to Alaska with his father and sister tomorrow night, is here with me.

Mayor Shy is dressed in jeans and a sparkly tank top, as if she's showing these spirits that they won't alter her life. However, I know different. She has been in touch with relatives in California and wants nothing more than to pack up Shelby-Nichole and get the hell out of Dodge . . . or Radisson, as the case may be. Civic duty and a promise to her deceased husband, Mayer, keeps her riveted in place as we try to rid this house of the troubled spirit that so needs to slip into the light and into eternal peace.

"We have one more person joining us tonight," Loreen says to me with a nudge in my side.

In the doorway stands my mother. Not Emily, but Sarah Moorehead. Her usual nurse's couture has been replaced by jeans and a Chicago Bears sweatshirt.

Our hands unite and she draws me to her. "I'm here for you, baby. Anything you need."

"Just you," I say muffled into her chest. "Don't be scared by what you might see tonight. I'm surrounded by my friends and the proper supervision. And now that you're here, Mom, I'm not so frightened."

"I love you so much, Kendall. I couldn't love you more if I had grown you in my belly. You're a part of me. You *are* my daughter."

"I know, Mommy."

Her free hand runs through my hair, which I've pulled back from my face with tiny clips. I have to be able to see everything clearly, whether it's psychically or for real. No surprises tonight. No beeyotch of a ghost is going to catch me off-guard again.

An hour later, we have plenty of temperature spikes, some EMF activity, and a handful of semi-discernible EVPs; however, no sign of Sherry Biddison.

Celia adjusts on the carpet next to me, setting her K-II meter on the floor and stretching her long legs out. "You know, this is the thing that all the millions of fans of the paranormal TV shows don't understand. You don't sit here for half an hour—twenty-two minutes if you take out the commercials—and get evidence upon evidence. This is tedious and often boring work."

Taylor clicks her tongue. "I prefer this to attempted murder on my friends."

Becca bites her bottom lip. "This might not be a popular thing to suggest, considering what happened the last time we were here, but I think we need to return to the upstairs landing. That's where Sherry showed herself before. I guarantee you we'll see her there again."

"I agree," Loreen says.

Reluctantly, I follow my group up the carpeted stairs, trying to cram down the creepy sensation slithering up my back.

No sooner do we get settled than Loreen begins to feel something. "She's near."

Well, then she needs to stay the hell away from me. I'm as locked up as a foreclosed home. I will not allow this spirit to enter me tonight. I will not grant her access to any part of my body, mind, or soul. All I can do is try to talk some sense into her if she shows herself.

"Kendall, are you going to attempt to channel?" Loreen asks.

"No," I say firmly. An apparition begins to take shape three feet in front of me. I squeeze my eyes shut, afraid to look at it

at first. Then I remember Emily's instructions, that I've got to
face this and do what God intended for me.

"Sherry Biddison," I begin. "I know you're here."

"Spike on the EMF," Celia reports.

Taylor adds, "I'm seeing streaks of light over there on the
infrared camera."

"Keep it up, Kendall." Loreen's encouragement warms me
and gives me daring.

"Talk to us, Sherry. Quit being such a royal bitch and just
tell me your story. You've hurt Mayor Shy, you've scared the
shit out of Shelby-Nichole, and you put me in intensive care
for four days. We're all women. Part of the sisterhood, ya know?
We can work this out."

Loreen's eyes roll up in her head and she begins to shake.
Bless her heart—she's taking on the channeling because she
knows I'm not physically strong enough for it. I can, however,
initiate the interview.

Scooting over to my friend, I ask, "Sherry, are you with us?"

The voice that leaves Loreen's lips isn't Loreen's at all. It's
scratchy and deeper. It's definitely Sherry Biddison in our midst.

"Why are you back?" Sherry bellows out, through Loreen.

"Because . . . we have unfinished business."

I see the temperature gauge on Celia's computer screen indicate a severe drop in the area. This ghost is doing her best to
manifest to me by using the energy around us.

"I'm tired. So . . . tired," she says.

I soften my approach. "Then let us help you."

"You'll just lock me up like they did," Sherry says.

"Who locked you up?"

"My parents did when I fell in love with a boy in town who had to go off and fight the war. I was with child and they were ashamed." Loreen rocks back and forth, moaning and groaning with Sherry's obvious burden. "They took my baby from me. They kept me hidden from the town."

Good God, people were horrible to each other back in the olden days. Would we still be locking one another up and stealing babies and such if we didn't have television, video games, and the Internet? How did we survive as a culture with such obsolete mores and codes governing our family lives? No wonder Sherry's pissed off at the entire human race. I suppose I would be too.

Then I think of my birth mother. Of Emily. Where was she going, all pregnant like that with me, so many years ago? Was she fleeing an abusive relationship? Was she ashamed of her predicament? Are people seriously that terrible to one another now?

I shake these thoughts out of my head. It's not about me right now. I'm starting to actually hurt for Sherry Biddison. The woman can only give what she received herself. Abuse, hatred, and suffering. These things begat more of the same in her life, it seemed.

"Sherry . . . how long did they have you locked up?"

Loreen's eyes shift about as if she—Sherry—is deciding whether to trust me or not.

"Please, Sherry."

"Six. Six years."

"Oh, dear Lord," Taylor says, clasping her hand over her mouth.

That's completely insane. I try to reach out with my psychic feelings to let Sherry know how appalled we are by this bit of news. It's not something you read in the annals of city history. Taint like that only gets covered up, hidden in a memory attic of its own.

"Who did this to you?"

"My own parents!"

"Okay, now that's just sick," Becca comments. I couldn't agree more.

Sherry's voice softens some as we're beginning to get to her. "It was only after the War of Northern Aggression that I was allowed outside. By then, I knew nothing of the outside world. The days of cotillions and handsome suitors were over. What lay ahead for the South was turmoil and the task of cleaning up the men's mess of war. We had very little food. No security in our lives. I returned to the attic, watching as a tattered town began to rebuild and wondering if I would ever find my place within it."

Loreen breathes heavily, gasping a bit as Sherry seems to be making herself comfortable in my friend's skin. Then Loreen's own voice breaks through. "Keep going, Kendall. You're helping."

Taylor continues to take pictures of Loreen using the burst mode on her camera. It's a bit of a psychotic photo shoot, but there's no telling what might materialize when we review it.

The closer I stare at Loreen, the more I see that it's not her face at all. It's the weathered, aged, bitter face of Sherry Biddison when she was older. The one who pushed me down the stairs in an attempt to end my life. I have to forgive her that, though. I honestly don't think she meant to harm me, per se. The malady of insanity still boils within, even in death.

Celia pipes up. "How did you come to be First Lady of this town that you so feared?"

Sherry's sadistic laugh tumbles from Loreen's lips. "Ahh-ha-ha-ha . . . arrangements of man. In an exchange for some very strategic farmland on the outskirts of the city, my own father traded me in near prostitution to a half-breed."

"An Indian?" Taylor asks.

"No! A half Yankee!"

Are we back to that? It's amazing America succeeded, with the regions of our country so divided. "Was he a Union soldier?"

Loreen bobs and weaves, catching herself with her palms on the floor. "Southern born. West Point educated. Served in the Twentieth Maine. Harlan Biddison. Came back to his roots to help the South rebound after she fell so ingloriously."

"There's a portrait of him in the formal dining room," Donn informs us. "He was known in our city records as a good and decent man."

I remember pieces of the story now. "And you had a son with him, right, Sherry?"

"Aye. My Harlan Jr. He was mine and no one was going to take him away from me. I overcame the madness to take care of him. He was my world."

Becca whispers low to me. "I'm sure he was one hell of a mama's boy."

"No kidding," Jason says.

"Shhh." I don't want anything to push Sherry away when we're so close with her. My heart aches with the suffering the woman experienced. Thuds in my chest reverberate into my head, causing an anvil of a migraine. It seems to press against my temporal lobe, squeezing out all logic and sensibility. "I need to think," I say.

My fingers fly to my temples, rubbing away at the empathic site. A doctor I'm not, but the diagnosis is becoming clear to me. Something is pressing against Sherry's brain. Certain blood vessels in the head aren't receiving enough oxygen, thus leading to her madness. Of course, it didn't help that her family locked her away. In later years, when she was a wife and mother, the pressure built on a daily basis, turning her into a deranged being.

Loreen's hands fly to her head as well. She rubs hard as if connected to what I'm picking up. Today, a CT scan could easily find the problem. Chemo, radiation, surgery, or even laser treatment might be able to destroy such a manifestation of runaway cell division.

In one simple word. "Cancer," I say in a hissed breath.

Celia flinches. "Poor woman. She had no clue about her madness."

"Apparently not." With all the energy I can allow my still-healing body to project, I mentally beg Sherry to show herself to me. In seconds, the transparent figure of the sad woman manifests before me.

"Ho. Ly. Shiite Muslim!" Celia exclaims. "I-I-I ... am I seeing what I think I'm seeing?"

"Très excellent!" Taylor joins in. She grabs her video camera and points it in the direction we are all—and I mean every single one of us in the room, including my mother, who gasps audibly—seeing the apparition of Sherry Biddison.

My mom speaks up. "Cancer would have been near impossible to diagnose properly in those days. From the talk of her madness, it could have been that the pressure was so intense in her skull from the tumor that she had no way to control her actions."

"Thanks, Mom." I face the apparition that is now taking full shape.

"She's there, right?" Celia asks.

"Yep. Your first. Welcome to my world."

Sherry apparently releases Loreen from the channeling session because Loreen collapses into Massimo's arms and startles awake.

"You're okay, Loreen," he says, so comfortingly. "I've got you."

Sherry Biddison has a captive audience. We are all paying rapt attention, watching her float about four inches off the ground. Donn's mouth hangs open, and Shelby-Nichole too moves in to get a better look. It's not every day a normal—nonsensitive—person is treated to an FBA. That's Celia tech talk for full-body apparition. (Okay, so she wasn't the one who coined it, but that's who I learned it from.)

"Why did you try to hurt your daughter-in-law, Virgilian?" I ask to the ghost's face.

Sherry frowns. "She took away my Harlan Jr."

"Not really," I note. "She only married him and gave him a child."

"He-he-he was all I had," she says, so eerily quiet that I get chill bumps on my arms. Only now do I realize that the tumor coupled with the madness of being locked away was more than Sherry could stand. With no medicine to help her, she gave in to her neurosis.

It's so clear to me. If we could have had this convo the last time we were here, I might not have been attacked and injured so badly. Then again, I wouldn't have had the experience with Grandma Ethel and Emily that I had. I wouldn't have learned the truth about my life. And I wouldn't have a future quest in life as strong as the one I have now.

"You have to forgive yourself, Sherry. You have to let go of the hatred. You have to release the hurt built up inside of you."

My team gathers around, everyone still in awe of the figure

before us. It's like no one is breathing or even thinking as they wait to see what is next.

Even now, it's apparent: Sherry trusts no one.

I walk toward her bravely, knowing she could very well take a pop at me again. "I understand what you're feeling, Sherry—I too have been lied to all of my life." I try not to look at Mom because I have no need to hurt her. However, her motherly eyes touch me and she smiles. She's aware of what I have to do here.

Another step in Sherry's direction. "You have to trust your family, though, to protect you and do the things they feel are in your best interest when you're too young to understand your-self. It may not seem right at the time—and I don't condone your parents locking you away—but you *must* forgive. Not only your parents but your husband for whatever his intentions were and your son for sharing his love with someone else."

Celia clears her throat slightly. "Ummm . . . like, hi, Sherry. Celia Nichols here. I did some research on Mayor Biddison and his son, who followed in his footsteps as a mayor of Radisson." Her hands shake nervously as she continues. "Did you know that the baby Virgilian was carrying was a little girl? She and Harlan Jr. named her Sherilyn, in your honor."

Sherry breaks down in tears. "Lord have mercy. After what I tried to do to her?"

"You were her family," I say. "She only wanted what was best."

An obviously moved Sherry puts her hands to her chest. "I wanted her to suffer the pain and heartache I'd felt. I'd done so many things wrong, and I suppose I wasn't responsible for everything I did—with this cancer you say I had. I am truly sorry for what I did to Virgilian. This is why I have been stuck in this manor. Day in and day out of watching happy families, needing them to be in as much pain as I was in. That was wrong of me."

Taylor wants to speak her mind all the same. "Life isn't one big party, ma'am. Neither is the dynamics of one family or another *la fin du monde*. The only thing that actually *is* the end of the world is . . . well, when the world ends." Taylor wipes her eyes with the back of her hand. Jason moves to her side so he's within hugging reach if necessary. "See, my mama tried to escape the pain she was going through. She took too much medication—we have that now in our time—and she ended up only hurting her children and herself more. She's now being put in an institution where she can be monitored and counseled so she doesn't do any harm to herself or anyone else again. With that, though . . . my brother and I are losing everything that's important in our lives."

Sherry nods. "I'm sorry for your mother, child."

"The point is," Taylor emphasizes, "that you're not alone, Sherry. Everybody hurts . . . sometimes. It's part of life."

"Thank you, REM," Becca says quietly.

Celia elbows her hard in the rib cage.

"May I?" Father Mass asks.

"Of course."

He crosses himself and closes his eyes in prayer for a moment. When his dark orbs land on our ghostly visitor, he says. "You're a woman of God, Sherry Biddison. I feel that about you."

"Aye, I am."

"Ask God for forgiveness. He will heal you and make you whole in his holy fellowship in heaven. All you have to do is let go and accept your death. Vengeance is not something that belongs to us. Let go of the confusion and hatred, Sherry. Go in peace and may the grace of God be with you. Now, and forevermore."

"Amen," we say as a group.

Immediately, the air becomes lighter; the scent of aged wool and mustier times recedes. Sherry is no longer before us and no longer with us. I know she has crossed into the light.

"We did it," I say to everyone.

"No, baby girl," Mom says. "You did it."

Sherry Biddison is now at peace. This house is at peace. Mayor Shy and Shelby-Nichole can continue living here and going on about their lives as usual. Most everyone can. Well, Jason and Taylor have to adjust to their new lives, but they're both smart and resilient. They'll do fine.

If only it could be that easy for me. Where do I go from here?

Mom wraps her arm around me as if she knows of my hesitation and internal doubt. Without question, I am loved and cherished by the Moorehead family—the only family I've ever known. Out there, somewhere, though, there are people who are part of me. People who I come from.

And like Sherry Biddison and most of the spirits the ghost huntresses have encountered, I *will* need answers.

Chapter Twenty

Monday morning, I awaken surprisingly early, considering the late hour our investigation ended.

There's no Emily there to rouse me with her motherly ways, and my own mom chose to let me sleep in.

However, in just a few hours, Taylor and Jason will be off to Alaska. As much as I hate it, it is what it is. It's reality.

I shower, shampoo, and shave my legs, and then take an extra long time blow-drying my hair and running the curling iron through it to get some body at the ends. I wand my eyelashes with a fresh tube of Lashblast and paint a smattering of lilac soufflé shadow on my lids. I dress in my cutest pair of Seven jeans—the ones with the sparklies across the butt pockets—and a red spaghetti-strap tank underneath a cropped black sweater. With one last glance in the mirror, a dusting of some gloss, and a slipping on of my Steve Madden mules, I'm ready to see my first boyfriend off on his new adventure.

Outside my house, Celia leans against my Honda Fit concentrating greatly on whatever she's manipulating on her BlackBerry.

"Word Mole?" I ask.

Her waggling tongue slips back into her mouth. "No. Sudoku."

"You still can't beat me," I say with a laugh.

"Yeah, well, that's why I practice."

I unlock the car doors and nod to the passenger side. "You coming with?"

"To Casa Tillson?" she asks.

"Where else."

We ride in conversational silence as an old-school best of Earth, Wind, and Fire CD spins out for us. I power the windows down, and we pace ourselves through the streets of Radisson, past the school and through the square over to Hancock Street. Number 305, to be precise. Ironically, just this morning, I looked up the meaning of this combination of digits in my Angel Numbers book:

God and ascended masters are guiding you through this Divine transition. All is well, and you are safe.

I don't know whether that speaks to Jason and Taylor or to me—perhaps to all of us. It's a good message that warms the cockles of the heart and gives me a sense of peace.

In front of the simple Colonial-style house, Taylor drags a rather large Louis Vuitton bag behind her. I had no idea they even made suitcases *that* large. Hope she knows that airlines charge for each piece of luggage these days.

Mr. Tillson relieves her of the load and swings the behemoth valise into the back of his rented SUV.

"Y'aaaaaaaaalllll," Taylor squeals when she sees us. The two of us are barely out of the car before our friend attacks us with a goodbye hug. Massive tears are shed by all of us. And you wonder why I didn't put on eyeliner this morning when I was fixing up.

"I'm going to miss you so badly, Tay-Tay," I say affectionately. Never have I ever met someone as popular and pretty as Taylor who is also as genuine and real.

"Me too," she says into my shoulder.

"You have our e-mails and cell phones," Celia says, like a mother sending her kid off to summer camp. "We can also IM and chat online just like we're across town from each other. Nothing has to change."

Tears shimmer in Taylor's eyes. "Y'all are the best friends I've ever had. Becca came by a little while ago and gave me this." Taylor tugs up the left leg of her jeans to reveal a tattoo of a small ghost on her ankle.

"You did not!" I say. "Becca did that?"

Taylor laughs heartily. "It's totally done in henna. But I think we should all get a real one. A symbol of our time together."

Celia's eyebrows lift. "Now *that's* an idea."

"I'm even thinking of starting my own ghost-hunting team once I get to Alaska," Taylor announces. "The one rule will be that nobody wears Uggs."

I laugh, knowing there's a pair of those ugly things in the way back of my closet.

Jason exits the house hauling a gigamonic duffle bag on his

shoulder. He looks just as gorgeous today as that first time I saw him in the school cafeteria after dreaming about him. No one on the planet has blue eyes to match his, and I'll never forget the way they stare at me with such affection.

"I think that's it," he says, hefting the bag into the vehicle.

"Are you bringing the kitchen sink too?" his dad asks.

"Humor me, Pop," Jason says. Then he turns to me and holds out his hand. "Come here, you."

I fall into step next to him as we walk to the other side of the car. Taylor and Celia continue to chat so that Jason and I can have a moment together.

He wraps his long arms around me and holds me so closely it seems like I'll be behind him at any second. His heartbeat strums in his chest that's pressed up against me, and I realize this is as hard for him as it is for me. This guy truly digs me.

"I love you so much, Kendall."

"I love you too, Jason. I always will."

His cool lips warm as they touch mine, parted slightly for the exhilaration of our final moment together as official girl-friend-boyfriend. The kiss deepens and intensifies to match the tumultuous emotions we're both feeling. For the first time, I sense Jason's thoughts directly. He's afraid to leave me at such a critical juncture in my life although there's nothing he can do about it. It feels to him like he's abandoning me.

I withdraw from the kiss, but not from him. "You're not abandoning me. You're keeping your family together. You and Tay need your dad right now. Your mom will get good medical care, and who knows what will happen. We have to stay positive, Jase."

His thumb brushes across my bottom lip in a whispered reverence. "You are always Ms. Susie Sunshine. That's one of the things I love about you, Kendall."

Yeah, well, it's all an act right now. I'm anything but positive about my own future. I just can't let on anything to Jason. He has to be assured that I'm okay so he can get on that airplane and fly off to the farthest reaches of our country. Family first— for both of us.

I lift up on my tiptoes to kiss him again. Soft and quick, over and over. "You'll always be in my heart, Jason Tillson."

"You too, K."

"You two done macking on each other over there?" Taylor calls out.

"Probably not," Celia remarks. "Anyone got a crowbar?"

"Har-har-har. Very funny," I say, still gripping Jason's hand.

"Like you and MacKenzie didn't make out for two hours last night," Jason says to his twin. "I should have broken his face."

Taylor punches at him. "Get over yourself."

"Right, Jason," Celia says. "All of those dogsledding boys are gonna loves them Miss Southern Belle."

We all laugh together and then fall into one giant embrace.

Mr. Tillson clears his throat. "I hate to break this up, kids, but Air Alaska waits for no one. Especially at the Atlanta airport."

One more hug. One more kiss. One more goodbye. And

then the Tillsons are backing out of their former driveway and disappearing around the curve.

"Hmm ..." Celia says, deep in thought.

"What?"

"Just wondering who we'll get to do photos for us now."

Now might not be the best time to tell her—although I owe her my honesty. "You may need to find someone to do the sensitive work as well."

"WTF? You can't ditch me too, Kendall! Are you moving back to Chicago?"

"No, not at all. I just need to . . . step away from the ghost hunting for a while."

"What about Emily?" Celia asks.

"She's gone," I say with a wistfulness in my voice.

"Like *gone* gone?"

I bob my head. All that time Emily and I spent together and I never realized she'd actually given birth to me. Wow . . . some psychic I've turned out to be. "She said she finally saw the light. For the first time since I was born. She had to go. I wanted nothing more than for her to stay, especially now that I have so many questions left unanswered."

"I'm sure." Celia reaches into her back pocket and pulls out some folded papers. "I wasn't sure if you'd still be interested in this. It's from my cousin Paul, with the GBI."

"About Emily?"

Celia's turn to bob her head. "Go ahead and peruse it."

My hand shakes as I read the report on missing person Emily Jane Faulkner, daughter of John Thomas and Anna Wynn Faulkner of St. Germain, Wisconsin. Last seen on December 21, 1993, at a Mobil station in Rockford, Illinois. Driving a Pontiac Grand Am registered in her name. Thought to be traveling from Wisconsin to St. Louis, Missouri, with Andy Caminiti . . .

I let my hands fall to my sides. "This has the names and locations of my real grandparents. And this Andy person—he could be my . . . father." The lump in my throat migrates down to my heart, causing it to beat like a locomotive. "Celia, do you know what this means?"

"We've got more investigations to carry out?"

"*I* do. I've got to find a way to get in touch with these people. I can't waste my energies anymore on strangers, Celia. Ghost hunting means nothing to me when it's possible there are people out there who can tell me about where I come from."

Seemingly confused, Celia asks, "Why is that so important to you?"

My mouth drops open. "It'll explain why I am the way I am. Why I'm . . . afflicted with this sixth sense. Why it's happening to me."

With hand extended, Celia says, "Anything I can do to help—count on me."

"Thanks. Maybe one day we'll get back to the ghost hunting."

Celia drops her chin into her chest; her dark hair covers her face. She digs her booted shoe into the gravel of the Tillsons' driveway and lets out a sigh. "All good things must come to an end."

With a snicker, I say, "So we've switched from Shakespeare to old English proverbs, eh?"

"Actually," she starts, "I was thinking of Jean-Luc Picard's final words on the last episode of *Star Trek: The Next Generation*."

I toss my head back and laugh like crazy for the first time in weeks. At least since my run-in with Sherry Biddison and her staircase of death. The jostling makes my side hurt where my surgery stitches have just been removed, but it's the best feeling in the world.

"You are *such* a geek. That's why I love you."

She flashes me a toothy grin and we begin walking back to my car.

"Besides," I say, "I *much* prefer Captain Kirk and the original series."

"Purist," she mutters.

"I call 'em as I see 'em."

"Why don't we start a *Star Trek* club at school," Celia suggests. She loops her long legs into my small car and buckles up. "We could have a convention and people can dress like their favorite character—you know, like cosplay. Or we could debate certain topics, like Romulan aggression versus Klingon independence. Maybe we could even try to do some time-travel experiments to see if we indeed need portals or if the slingshot around the sun works."

As Celia Nichols, queen of the science geeks, prattles on, I shift gears and smile. Sure, our ghost-huntress team is in a little disarray, but nothing will stop girls with a mission.

That we are!

EPILOGUE

I SIT AT RADISSON'S CENTRAL PERK CAFÉ stirring my chai soy latte—I know, how pretentious-sounding of me—and let out a long sigh. God willing, I've just aced the last of my midterms and am almost done with calculus in my life ... forevah.

Spring break is coming up in a few weeks. Celia, Taylor, Becca, and I were going to drive down to Destin, with Loreen and my mom chaperoning, and do a little ghost hunting. That's off the table now.

I got a text from Taylor yesterday telling me how gorgeous Alaska is and how she's never seen so many people wearing plaid, which she finds goes well with her American Eagle jeans that make her butt look cute—her words, not mine. Leave it to Taylor Tillson to take the lemons and not only make lemonade but have enough left over for lemon teacakes and lemon chiffon pie.

Mmmm ... pie. Maybe I'll get a piece to celebrate finishing my tests.

If only life were so simple that a mere dessert could assuage all aches.

And I am sadly hurting. A dull throbbing daily that has me tossing and turning in my sleep. It's more than just losing Jason and seeing him and Taylor move off. It's the uncertainty of so many things. My existence, for starters.

I stare at the foam in my cup as if it's an apparition of my past. I wish it could answer my questions. Before, I was just Kendall Moorehead, daughter of David and Sarah, from Chicago, Illinois. Now, I'm the adopted daughter of a kind nurse and a dedicated city planner. They're still my parents; that's a no-brainer. However, deep down, in a crevice of my stomach, that groaning sensation gurgles, stirring up the endorphins in my brain, which has more questions than a Trivial Pursuit game.

Sure, looking back at the past few months of my life, see I've experienced more than most "normal" teenagers do. My psychic awakening is now nothing compared to having a near-death experience and then finding out I'm adopted.

I miss Emily terribly. At times, it seems she's still watching over me, but I know that's just a pipe dream. She finally found her peace where she belongs. When will I find mine, though? I've stared at that piece of paper Celia gave me from her cousin a hundred times. The names write out in cursive in my mind's eye.

Emily Jane Faulkner.

John Thomas and Anna Wynn Faulkner.

Andy Caminiti.

Significant players in the movie of my life.

My dreams are fraught with myriad images of strangers. A gray-haired woman sitting on a back porch, watering flowers. An older man with a hearing aid casting for fish on a lake. A woman making breakfast for a large group of people in a mountain resort. Mountains, too, color my dreams. Beautiful, majestic rocks shooting high into the vast blue sky, as if reaching to heaven. Waterfalls of misty streams fall between boulders casting off prisms of rainbows. It's a gorgeous place, but I have no idea where it is or why I'm seeing visions of it.

And then there's the guy. The one I've dreamed of before. Dark blackish brown hair with streaks of gray or white at the temples. Jet-black eyebrows and eyes the color of coffee before it's diluted with cream. He bores those chocolate eyes into me as if there's hatred or resentment between us—which is wicked sad 'cause he's wicked cute. Who he is, I haven't a clue, but knowing how things are for me since my awakening, I'm sure I'll meet him soon.

Mom's Volvo pulls up to the curb and she honks the horn as she waves. I nab my Styrofoam cup, book bag, and purse and head out.

"Calculus?" she asks when I open the car door.

"Ninety-seven."

Mom holds up her hand, wanting a high-five. Since she's not aware that kids my age fist bump instead, I humor her. "I'm so proud of you, Kendall," she says.

"Thanks, Mom. I'm proud of me, too—considering all the crap I've been through."

She places her hand lovingly on my knee and squeezes. "That's something I wanted to talk to you about. Dig into my purse and pull out that stuff I printed."

I bend and find several pages stapled together. Enlightened Youth Retreats? I read. "What's this for?"

Mom glances over and then back at the road as she drives through Radisson toward our house. "I called Dr. Ken Kindberg in Atlanta, remember him?"

"Sure." Dr. Kindberg was the psychiatrist who confirmed that I do indeed possess the psychic skills I claim to have. "Why did you call him?" Probably a stupid question, considering . . . everything.

Mom rolls her eyes at me and snickers. "Annnnnyway. I filled him in on all you have been through lately and he directed me to this website that can help you."

My heart falls a bit. What website can assist a girl who loses her first love? Who now has a blistering red scar from having her spleen removed? Who's too afraid to connect with the spirit world she's been dealing with for seven months? Who wants nothing more than to beg for medication to get her to stop having psychic visions and empathic headaches? I need a website where I can put in my name and my birth mother's name and out will spew all the pertinent backstory so I'll know who I am.

"Kendall, hon . . . just read it."

I let my eyes dance over the page, reviewing information about teens just like me who are considered to be "enlightened." Psychics, mediums, indigo children, empathics, healers, telepaths, and others who have special gifts and abilities. I read aloud. "'Nestled in the backyard of Yosemite National Park is Rose Briar Inn, the site of our year-round Enlightened Youth Retreats. Here, specially gifted young people from ages thirteen through twenty can gather together for seminars, lectures, hands-on experiments, meditation, and quiet time with others or nature in the relaxing town of Oakbriar, California.'"

My eyes pop. "California?"

"Yes," Mom says. "Since your spring break is coming up, your dad and I thought this would be a good thing for you."

"A retreat, huh?" Cali-frickin'-fornia!

"Right, dear. The cost covers all of your meals and housing, and you'd meet others from all over the country who have similar gifts as yours. I know you've been feeling disjointed lately and perhaps this trip is just what the doctor ordered."

"Or the nurse," I say with a smile.

"The nurse definitely recommends it," Mom says. "As much as I'll hate having you away from home for ten days, your father and I feel like this is the best thing for you, Kendall."

"Won't airfare be kind of expensive?"

Mom winks at me. "Kendall, don't worry about things like that Your father and I aren't struggling and we want our girls to be happy. This is what you need. Time away from Radisson and your ghost hunting—which you already said you wanted a break from—and a chance to meet other teens like you."

A week in the Sierra Nevadas, huh? A mountain getaway? An opportunity to find out who Kendall Moorehead really is before I delve into the mystery that *is* my mother . . . and my family.

"I think I'll do it!" I say to Sarah, my mother.

"Good! Your dad and I can make all the arrangements this evening. And you know what one of the coolest things is? That psychic from TV, Oliver Banks—the guy who wears the Ray-bans all the time when he's getting psychic messages on that true-crime show—is the one who runs it and helps kids just like you."

My brow hitches. "*You* watch a TV show about a psychic that solves true crimes?"

Mom hems and haws. "Oh, you know. It's one of those things on at night . . . background noise that I stop on occasionally."

She is the cutest thing evah! Considering she wanted to medicate me at first when my psychic abilities blossomed. I'm proud of her accepting my gift—or my curse, whichever way you might see it.

Perhaps this retreat will do the trick.

We pull into our driveway, and Mom parks the car. I lean over and kiss her on the cheek. "Love ya; mean it."

I do mean it. She may not have physically birthed me, but she is my mother. She cares enough about me to let me explore and find myself.

And I will. There will be plenty of time for that after spring break.

Time for Kendall Moorehead to discover the truth of her roots.

First off, California, here I come!

To be continued . . .

DISCLAIMER

The thoughts and feelings described by the character of Kendall are typical of those experienced by young people awakening to sensitive or psychic abilities.

Many of the events and situations encountered by Kendall and her team of paranormal investigators are based on events reported by real ghost hunters. Also, the equipment described in the book is standard in the field.

However, if you are a young person experiencing psychic phenomena, talk to an adult. And while real paranormal investigation is an exciting, interesting field, it is also a serious, sometimes even dangerous undertaking. While I hope you are entertained by the Ghost Huntress, please know that it's recommended that young people not attempt the investigative techniques described here without proper adult supervision.

BIBLIOGRAPHY

Attunement-activation healing with sounds and energy information courtesy of Chuck Reynolds, 10705 Newgate Lane, Indianapolis, IN 46231; www.attunementactivation.com.

Ovilus information via Bill Chappell, inventor of the tool. For more information, visit http://www.digitaldowsing.com.

This version of St. Michael's Prayer courtesy of discussion with Archbishop James Long of the Paranormal Clergy Institute, who is an exorcist and demonologist. He explains that it's not as important to recite the exact prayer as it is to get across the intent of the prayer, to protect yourself with the help of God's angels. He can be found at http://www.paranormalclergy.com.